LEARNING
TO
FALL

SALLY ENGELFRIED

LITTLE, BROWN AND COMPANY
New York   Boston

Little, Brown and Company
Hachette Book Group
1290 Avenue of the Americas, New York, NY 10104
Visit us at LBYR.com

First Edition: September 2022

Little, Brown and Company is a division of Hachette Book Group, Inc. The Little, Brown name and logo are trademarks of Hachette Book Group, Inc.

The publisher is not responsible for websites (or their content) that are not owned by the publisher.

Library of Congress Cataloging-in-Publication Data
Names: Engelfried, Sally, author.
Title: Learning to fall / Sally Engelfried.
Description: First edition. | New York : Little, Brown and Company, 2022. | Audience: Ages 8–12. | Summary: Daphne spends a vacation with her estranged father, whom she has not seen in years, and the pair bond over their love of skateboarding.
Identifiers: LCCN 2021057421 | ISBN 9780316367974 (hardcover) | ISBN 9780316368285 (ebook)
Subjects: CYAC: Fathers and daughters—Fiction. | Family problems—Fiction. | Alcoholism—Fiction. | Skateboarding—Fiction. | LCGFT: Fiction.
Classification: LCC PZ7.1.E5295 Le 2022 | DDC [Fic]—dc23
LC record available at https://lccn.loc.gov/2021057421

ISBNs: 978-0-316-36797-4 (hardcover), 978-0-316-36828-5 (ebook)

Printed in the United States of America

LSC-C

Printing 1, 2022

For David

1

Where was he?

The sign above my head said PASSENGER PICKUP, so I knew I was in the right place. I couldn't believe this was happening again.

The knot of worry that had been sitting in my gut all morning tightened every time someone got into a car. Why did Mom think we could trust him to be here? My flight landed half an hour ago. I pulled my phone out of my back pocket, but then I remembered Mom was still on the plane to Prague. Calling her wouldn't do any good.

I looked up and down the pickup area for the

thousandth time. Should I call my grandparents? Mom told me to contact them in case of an emergency. Being stranded at the Oakland Airport was an emergency, wasn't it? I started scrolling through my contacts. Right when I found their number, a horn beeped and a beat-up blue Toyota skidded to a stop at the curb next to me. My dad popped out of the driver's side, a huge grin on his face.

I slowly slid my phone back into my pocket, staring at him. It had been so long since I'd seen him. He looked the same, minus the scruffy beard he used to have.

"Daphne!" he called across the car roof, waving wildly like I might not notice him if he didn't.

I couldn't seem to move.

He slammed the car door and ran over, throwing his arms around me. "Daf!" he murmured into my hair. "It's so good to see you." I stood there while he squeezed me, my arms pinned to my side.

I didn't say a word.

He finally let go, and I took a step back to put more space between us. "I can't believe you're twelve years old already," he said, smiling.

Was I supposed to be impressed he knew how old I

was? I tried to give him the Cold Fish, which involves leaning your head slightly to the right, raising your eyebrows a little, and making your eyes as dead as possible, but my dad's eyes were so wide and excited, as if my face was the best, most amazing thing he'd ever seen. It made my stomach dip in a way it hadn't for a while.

I turned away and studied the sea of cars in the parking lot, blinking my eyes a bunch of times. *Three years*, I reminded myself. *Three years and the only reason he's here is because Mom needs a babysitter.*

I turned back when he grabbed the handle of my rolling suitcase. "I'll get this," he said. He looked down at my hands and then up at my face. "No board, huh?"

"Nope." This time I did manage the Cold Fish. "I don't skate anymore."

"Oh." The brightness in his eyes dimmed. Then he flashed his single dimple at me, the same one that showed up on my face when I smiled. "I've got an extra board at the house if you want to get back into it." He slung my suitcase into the hatchback. "What do you think?"

I shrugged, my eyes on the ground. My dad cleared his throat. "Well, hop in. We're about twenty minutes from home."

In the car he drummed his hands on the steering wheel as he waited for the light to change at the airport exit. "So you don't dominate at the parks? Show off your sick tricks?"

"Nope." The word squeezed out of my lips, flat and expressionless. "No tricks."

I stared out the passenger window, but he kept trying. "Grandma and Grandpa are really looking forward to seeing you."

"Oh." I hadn't really thought about my grandparents being part of this trip until Mom programmed their numbers into my phone. I was supposed to call them if I saw my dad drink any alcohol whatsoever, "even so much as a sip of beer," Mom insisted.

"We're having dinner with them tomorrow night."

"Okay." Maybe I wasn't thrilled to be here with my dad, but it might be nice to see my grandparents again. It had been so long, I couldn't even picture their faces. But they sent me a card with a crisp fifty-dollar bill every birthday and Christmas. Mom liked to remind me that "just because they send you money doesn't mean you owe them anything," but I figured it meant they must care about me, at least a little.

"So the house is kind of a mess. I'm still working on it." My dad was still trying to make conversation.

"It's fine." I sensed him glancing at me, but I kept staring out the window. I hadn't expected Oakland to look so different from Los Angeles. The sky here was a different color—wisps of white clouds making the blue even bluer, compared with the yellowy brightness of L.A. If Mom was here, we'd try to figure out what else made it different: Were the houses closer together? Were the trees greener? But it was my dad, so I just stared and wondered on my own until he pulled up in front of a small house with a wide porch and peeling green paint.

"Yeah," he plowed on, "I think this place'll end up being pretty nice. Your grandparents were so happy I finally . . . Well, anyway, they helped me get the house. I could never afford to live here if they hadn't."

"Nice," I muttered. They *gave* him a house? Did he know about all the times Mom had to beg our house-mates for an extension on the rent, or that time a few years ago when we had to sleep on her friend Sheri's pull-out couch for two months?

My dad kept talking. "It's a fixer-upper, nothing fancy. My friend Gus is a contractor, and he lives next door. We have a deal: I'm helping him work on his house first, and then he's going to help me. But when I heard a couple of months ago you were coming, we switched it so we could fix up your room first. It's all done."

"A couple of months ago?" I said, startled out of my Cold Fish. "But Mom just got the part."

"Right." He drummed his fingers on the steering wheel again and glanced over at me, then looked quickly away. "Well, I was hoping she'd get it."

"Oh." That was strange. As far as I knew, he and Mom only talked that minute before Mom handed her phone over to me for the awkward conversation I'd been having with my dad once a month for the past two years. My stomach dipped again with a sudden missing of Mom and home. It felt wrong to be staying with this dad I barely knew, in a room that was mine but I'd never seen before, having dinner with grandparents I could hardly remember.

But it didn't matter how much I missed Mom or our little apartment. She wasn't home, and we'd sublet our place to an actor friend of hers. As mad as I was at her for sending me away, I really did get it: It was huge that she'd gotten this movie part. It was going to change our lives, she said.

Besides, soon enough I'd be right there with her in Prague, and I wouldn't have to deal with staying with my dad.

My dad didn't say anything as he led me up the path to the porch. He fumbled with his keys. He dropped them twice. When he finally got the door open, he looked over his shoulder and smiled. I followed him inside, realizing something. I'd never been anywhere my dad lived. He'd always picked me up, or Mom dropped me off to meet him somewhere. It made this whole situation seem even more strange.

My black Vans scuffed the wood floor of the small living room. It had the air of not really being settled yet—there was a shabby brown couch and a bookcase, a few cardboard boxes stuffed into the corner, and a stack of framed pictures leaning against the wall. My dad let out a stiff laugh as he walked me through the kitchen, which was small and dark with an ugly yellowy-green stove. "I'll redo this one of these days. I'm not much of a cook, but even I can see how hideous it is." When I didn't say anything, his smile faded. He led me down the hall. He pointed to one door. "Bathroom." Then to the one next to it. "My room." Then he opened a door at the end of the hall. "And here's your room."

I couldn't hold back a gasp of amazement.

It was huge.

I'd never had a bedroom to myself before. Mom and I moved around a lot. Until recently we'd always shared a room in a house with other people, so when we got our own one-bedroom apartment last year, it was a thrill just to be by ourselves. We'd put up a curtain to divide the bedroom so we each had our own space. Now that Mom was getting some money from this movie, we'd talked about getting a bigger place sometime soon.

But *this*? This big square room filled with light? It belonged to me right now? I stood in the center and slowly turned around to take in every inch of this space that was mine for as long as I had to stay here. One wall was painted a deep, dark blue, the color of night sky. The others were a soft white, and one had a large, square window that looked into the backyard. A small table stood on one side of the bed, with a low bookshelf on the other. I sat down on the bed and bounced gently, thinking of my single mattress on the floor at home. My best friend, Samantha, thought it was cool that I got to sleep on the floor, but I envied her big double bed with its metal frame.

My dad stepped in behind me. "Your grandma stopped me from getting all pink bedding. I remember you used to like that, but she said you would have outgrown it by now." I ran my hand over the bedspread, which had stripes of silky dark purple and dark blue velvet. "Then I thought about painting all the walls different colors, but I figured white would keep it nice and bright, and you can put pictures up if you want. Or you can repaint if you don't like the blue. What do you think?"

Cold Fish, I reminded myself, looking around, conscious of my dad watching me. Did he think a pretty bedroom would erase all the time we hadn't spent together? "It's all right," I said flatly. I walked over to the window to avoid looking at him. The truth was, I had already fallen fully in love with the room. But no way would I admit it. I pretended to study the yard even though it was only a bunch of weeds with some broken lawn furniture.

A loud *scrape-slam! scrape-slam!* came from somewhere nearby. My heart sped up to match its rhythm. "What's that?"

My dad stepped next to me. "That? Oh, that's Gus's bowl."

"Bowl?"

"Yeah, his skate bowl. He has one in his backyard. You'll see it later today. I'll lend you a board. A bunch of us go over there to skate every Tuesday. Silver Bowl Sesh, we call it." My dad tapped the gray hair sprinkled at his temples. "Because of us skaters getting so old."

A skate bowl right next door? I pressed my ear to the cool glass. That *sound*. There was something so satisfying about it, so right, like something clicking into place. The old feeling rose in me, from the soles of my Vans up to my brain. My fingers twitched with the urge to grab a skateboard and make that sound myself.

"Pretty cool, right?" My dad's excitement reminded me to hide my own.

"I guess," I said.

From the front of the house, a voice called out. "Joe! You home?"

"Who's that?" I turned from the window.

"Must be Gus. Probably wants to borrow a tool. Come on, I'll introduce you."

He was already in the hall, but I stayed a second longer. I was hoping to hear the sound again, but it had stopped.

I let out a little sigh and went to meet this Gus person.

2

A tall guy in paint-spattered overalls stood in the front doorway, asking my dad if he could borrow something called a multimeter. "Told Rusty I'd fix up her car stereo for her. Oh, hey, Daphne!" Gus had light brown skin and thick black hair that curled over his forehead. His smile took over his whole face, with those crinkly lines at the corner of his eyes that meant he was the kind of person who smiled a lot. "I haven't seen you since you were about this high!" He lifted his hand to his hip.

I stared at him, startled. I had no memory of this guy.

"Looks like you went ahead and grew up." He

chuckled, then leaned back out the front door and yelled, "Hey, Arlo! Come over here for a sec!"

A minute later a boy appeared at his shoulder. "Arlo, this is Joe's daughter, Daphne," Gus said. "You guys are the same age. It's so cool that you'll both have someone to hang out with this summer!"

Seriously? Mom would never expect me to be friends with her friend's kid just because we happen to be the same age.

"Hey," Arlo said. He had the same coloring as Gus, and his shoulders hunched over in that way tall kids sometimes did, trying to be shorter. "It's a well-known fact that being the same age is a great basis for a deep and meaningful friendship."

I laughed. I didn't mean to, but I liked the slow, sarcastic way Arlo said it. My dad's face lit up, and Gus smiled again too. Great. Now I had them thinking I was fine with all this, that I was the kind of kid who would make the best of being thrust into any situation—new house, new friend, whatever.

The thing was, that *was* how I was, usually. Mom liked to brag to her friends that I was the easiest-going kid on the planet. But with my dad I couldn't unclench my jaw or the tight little ball that sat in the middle of my stomach. I didn't feel easygoing, not at all. But even more, I didn't *want* to be. Why should I?

My dad said, "There's some lemonade in the fridge, Daf. You and Arlo help yourselves. And to anything else you see in there if you want. I have to dig up my multimeter. It's in the garage somewhere." He and Gus went outside, and Arlo and I stared at each other.

"Yak Face, right?" I said, pointing to his T-shirt.

He raised his eyebrows at me, clearly impressed. "You're a *Star Wars* geek too?"

I laughed. "Not really." When it was Sam's turn to pick something for our movie nights with Mom, she always chose one of those. I liked to complain that there were ninety million of them, but I didn't really mind. "Um, you want some lemonade?" I asked.

"Sure." He followed me into the kitchen. I opened three cabinet doors looking for drinking glasses until Arlo opened the one near the sink and pulled out two.

I watched him open the fridge and pull out the lemonade. "I guess you and your dad have been here before," I said.

He raised one eyebrow at me. "Gus is my mom's boyfriend. Not my dad."

"Oh, I thought—" I stopped.

"That we're both brown, so we must be related?"

My cheeks got hot. "No, I didn't mean—"

Arlo laughed. "It's cool. My dad is Mexican, and Gus is too. First Latino guy my mom's dated since my dad, and he doesn't even know Spanish."

"Do you?" I asked, relieved he wasn't offended.

"Sí, por supuesto," he said. "But my mom doesn't, and I'm getting out of practice. I like to be able to talk to my abuela when I visit her and my dad in Arizona. Guess I have to break down and take it in school next year to make sure I don't forget it completely. I'm starting seventh grade. You too?"

"Yeah." I sipped my lemonade.

"So your mom is, like, a movie star or something?"

Hah. She'd love that. I leaned back against the sink. "No, not yet. She's an actor though."

"Your dad was bragging about her."

He brags about her? I didn't even know he kept track of Mom's career. "She just got a good part. In a big-budget movie. She's on a plane to the Czech Republic right now, in fact."

"Right. I've heard it's cheaper to film there," Arlo

said. I nodded, surprised he knew that. "How about you? You an actor too?"

"Me? No way!"

Arlo almost choked on his gulp of lemonade, laughing at my horror. "That bad, huh?"

"I think there's only room for one actor in the family."

"How come?" Arlo asked.

I thought about all the auditions Mom went to that didn't amount to anything, the dark moods she fell into afterward, and the sniffling I'd hear in the middle of the night that meant she was crying but didn't want me to know. "I don't know," I said. "Acting takes a lot of energy. My mom is obsessed with it."

"I get it. My mom's got an obsession too." He paused dramatically. "Boyfriends!"

I laughed, but Arlo said, "No, really. Whatever the guy gets into, we get into."

I eyed him. He was acting as if it was a joke, but the edge to his voice told me he didn't find it all that funny. "Like what?" I asked.

"Well, in the past two years she's been interested in"—he counted off on his fingers—"rescuing pit bulls, investing in the stock market, fishing, and accordion music. Now it's skating, of course."

I widened my eyes. "Your mom skates?"

"Nah," he said, shaking his head. "She took a few lessons, but she gave up pretty quickly. She mostly cheers Gus on and tries really hard to get me to bond with him since I skate too. It's annoying, but it's way better than watching those accordion bands!" He mimed squeezing an accordion and did a silly little jig that made us both laugh.

"How about you?" Arlo asked when our laughter died out. "Your dad's a pretty rad skater. You must be into it too, right?" He nodded at my clothes. I looked down at myself and realized my mistake. I was wearing my usual oversized T-shirt, baggy Ben Davis long shorts, and Vans. Maybe I should have borrowed some of Sam's retro, thrift store dresses for the summer, because I seemed to fit right in with my dad. And I didn't. Not at all. But I didn't want to ruin the friendly mood with Arlo. I shrugged vaguely and asked if he was going to be at Gus's that night.

"You mean the Old Man Skate Sesh?" he asked.

"Uh, I think my dad called it something else?"

"Yeah." Arlo laughed. "I just like to give them a

hard time. Those guys are way too old to be that into skating. I'll be there. How about you?"

"I guess."

"It's cool. They're good skaters even if they are ancient. I've been filming them some." He adjusted the strap that crossed his chest and gave the camera case that hung from it a gentle pat. "I'm taking a film-making class over the summer. When I told Gus about it, he showed me a bunch of classic skate movies, *Dogtown and Z-Boys*, Spike Jonze, stuff like that. It kind of inspired me."

I wanted to ask more—I'd never heard of that movie—but outside a woman's voice called, "Arlo! It's time to go!"

"My mom." He stood up. "See you later."

"See you later," I repeated.

After Arlo and Gus left, my dad poured himself a glass of lemonade and sat down. "You and Arlo seem to hit it off. It'll be good to have a friend for the summer, right?"

"I just met him. We're not *friends*." The part of me that had loosened a little talking with Arlo turned back to wood again. If my dad thought I was okay with being here because I had one conversation with the boy next door, he was wrong. I wasn't planning on being here long enough to make friends anyway. "Can I go to my room? I want to text Mom."

My dad scratched the back of his neck. "She's still on her flight, isn't she?"

Dang. I didn't think he'd know that. "I want her to get my message right when she lands."

"Right. Sure." He nodded, but as I left the kitchen, he was frowning and staring down at the table, his lemonade untouched.

Not my problem.

I pulled out my phone and thumped down onto the bed, anger rising up again. I tapped out a message to Mom:

> I still can't believe you left
> me here with someone I
> barely know 😡

I shoved the pillows against the headboard—three of them, all big and fluffy, with cases that matched the bedspread. I leaned back and crossed my arms over my chest. I looked around the room—*my* room—and thought about describing it to Sam. Sam's parents were divorced too, so she got that it was complicated between me and my dad. Still, I didn't think I could explain how much I truly loved this room but how it also made me angry at him.

I looked up. The vast white ceiling above me and the huge soft bed below me, the window with sunshine streaming through—together they somehow made me feel I had more space *inside* myself too. I let out a sigh and uncrossed my arms. Maybe I could avoid any more awkward conversations with my dad by just hanging out in this room until my plan came through.

I picked up my phone again and tapped out another text to Mom.

> **Did you ask them yet? When can I come and visit you?**

There was no reason my plan shouldn't work. I'd been on sets before, after all. I knew how to be quiet and inconspicuous, to stay in the trailer until someone told you it was okay to come out.

But I didn't hit SEND. I already felt a little guilty for the angry text before.

When Mom had gotten the part in the movie, we'd both screamed and danced around our living room. We were so loud that our neighbor came over to make sure everything was okay. Later, when I asked her if I could go to Prague too, Mom told me she didn't want to ask for anything that might make people think she was hard to work with. It was a couple of days after that when she told me I was going to my dad's. I was so mad at her! She promised she'd figure something out, but I had to give her time. I let out a sigh and deleted my questions.

> Lmk when you land! And tell me when you meet some movie stars! Wait! I forgot you don't need to meet them—you're one of them now! 😉

She'd like that. I'd ask her about coming to Prague later.

Scrape-slam! Someone was skating next door again. I lay back on the pillows and closed my eyes. The sound of skateboard wheels clattering on the bowl next door lulled me to sleep.

3

A knock on the door made me bolt up. I grabbed my phone to check the time. Four o'clock already? "Yeah?" I said, trying not to sound sleepy.

My dad poked his head in the door and glanced around. Was he thinking I already decorated it or something? I decided right then not to do anything to my room that would make him think I'd settled in. Why bother when I'd be leaving soon anyway? "Time to head to Gus's. You ready?"

I shrugged.

"Daphne. Please come. I've been telling everyone

about you." He huffed a sigh of frustration—quiet, but I heard. "They really want to meet you. Gus and Rusty are making tacos for all of us after. Please?"

From the hopeless way he asked, I could tell that if I said I didn't want to go, he'd close the door and let me stay in my room all night. But suddenly the prospect of spending the entire night completely alone didn't seem that great. Besides, I kind of wanted to see Gus's bowl. I'd never heard of anyone having one in their backyard before. I swung my legs onto the floor. "I guess I can go," I mumbled, as if I was doing him a huge favor.

We were almost out the door when he said, "Oh! Almost forgot!" He disappeared down the hall and came back with a skateboard and a helmet. He shoved the board at me. "Here, you can use this one." I stepped back, away from his offering. So many words crowded into my mouth. I couldn't get any of them out.

"In fact"—he jiggled the board—"you can have it. The helmet too. Use them all summer. Take them home with you if you want. You must have outgrown that one I got you for your birthday, right?" He smiled as if it was something to be proud of, the fact that he gave me a birthday present three years ago.

My cheeks warmed, and some of those words

almost pushed their way out: *You mean, the last time I saw you? The board you promised to teach me how to ride? The board I swore never to ride again after what happened?* But I just pressed my lips together and lowered my eyes. "I'm not taking it." I edged by him, my hands clenched into fists at my sides.

I stalked out the front door but didn't know where to go, so I had to wait till he came out. I followed him across the dried-up lawn to the gate next door. Music blasted from the backyard, and as my dad reached over the fence to lift the latch, I heard a whoop and a hammering that started my heart pounding. "What's that?" I asked.

"Someone must've landed their trick." My dad grinned. "The guys watching hit their boards on the deck. It's an appreciation thing. You'll see."

The music and the scrape and screech of skate wheels got louder as we walked through an ordinary backyard with trees and tall flowering plants that spilled over a stone path. I couldn't see the bowl, but my heart lifted with each step that brought us closer to that noise.

At the back of the yard a ladder leaned against a short wall. "Let's head on up," my dad said, raising his voice. At the top, my eyes fixed on the skater in the bowl, and my breath caught in my throat. I vaguely noticed the people standing around the edge.

"Daf, come on. We can't stand here."

I couldn't stop watching. It was Gus. After a minute I realized I'd let my dad grab my hand and lead me to a corner. I pulled it away and watched Gus ride up to the coping on the lip of the bowl. He launched himself out of the bowl, one hand grabbing the middle of his board, the other on the coping. And then he turned *upside down*, his feet somehow still attached to his board as it tipped into the air. He swooped back down and landed in the bowl.

"Wow," I breathed. And just as my dad had said, all the guys started banging their boards on the coping, grins on their faces.

"Frontside invert," my dad told me. "Pretty good, right? He's been working on it for a while." I nodded, my eyes still glued to the bowl. A guy on the other side dropped in.

"Come on, Daf. I want to introduce you to people."

I glanced around. Arlo was on the other side, and we waved to each other. To the right of us, a guy with long black hair stood waiting his turn, his board tipped up in his hand. Colorful tattoos wrapped around his arms, too many to make out. He turned when my dad yelled over the music, "Diego, this is Daphne."

My dad put his hand on my shoulder, like the guy wouldn't be able to figure it out. I wriggled out of my dad's grip.

"Hi," I said. Diego smiled at me, and I was glad to see that it was as hard for him to keep his eyes off the bowl as it was for me. We all turned back to watch.

My dad pointed at the guy riding up and down the bowl. "Isaiah's our rising star," he said.

Gus's trick had been really cool, but Isaiah had an extra grace, his board like an extension of his feet. "See how he keeps his shoulders loose and they move along with his board? That's key," my dad said into my ear, and I nodded—it was exactly what I had been noticing—and it rushed back to me, the solid feeling of my dad next to me at skate parks when I was little, before I had my own board. I remembered how my insides would lift as the skaters landed their tricks, so that I imagined a tiny skate bowl inside my stomach. My dad would talk about their form, just as he was doing now, the tricks and terms rolling off his tongue. Back then I loved to repeat them over and over in my head, almost like a prayer: *Ollie, nollie, kickflip, shuvit. Backside, frontside, fakie, grind.* I clenched my jaw. That was a long time ago. I pushed the refrain out of my head.

"Isaiah's actually so good, us old guys get a little intimidated," my dad was saying, unaware I'd slipped back in time for a minute. "Tyler over there owns a skate shop." He pointed across the bowl to a guy with a bushy, gray-streaked beard watching Isaiah with intense concentration. "He's working on getting Isaiah some sponsor deals. Niiice!" my dad called out as Isaiah popped up on the coping right near our feet. "Frontside 5-0," my dad told me. Isaiah shot him a grin and kept going. My dad stopped talking, and we both watched until Isaiah popped onto the deck and gave Arlo the nod.

I watched Arlo drop into the bowl, curious about how he'd compare with these guys who'd been doing it for years but who were...well, pretty old, except Isaiah, and even he was still a grown-up. Arlo wasn't as smooth as Isaiah, but he could definitely skate. He carved around the bowl a couple of times, then rode up onto the coping and straddled his wheels over it in a 50-50 grind. He kick turned but pitched forward off his board on the way down. I sucked in my breath, embarrassed for him, but Arlo just laughed and ran back up the transition to stand next to me.

Diego dropped in and skated for a while, and then because I was in the spot where he'd waited, he gave me the subtle chin lift that meant it was my turn.

I shook my head, *so* glad I didn't have a board. Then Arlo pushed his board into my hand. "Go ahead," he said. I pushed it back at him. "No!" I said, my voice so shrill it rose over the music. Arlo looked confused. Behind me my dad said, "Daphne?"

I pushed past Arlo, panic filling me. I had to get out of there! Away from the bowl. Away from everyone. But someone was standing in front of me, and I couldn't get around him.

"I'm up!" my dad called out. I turned around as he dropped in. My shoulders sagged in relief. Everyone was watching my dad skate as if nothing had happened. Maybe they hadn't noticed my overreaction at the mere idea of dropping in. But Arlo was looking at me. He raised his eyebrows. I shrugged and shot him a half-hearted smile. We both turned back to the bowl.

I hadn't seen my dad skate since I was a kid, when I thought he was the best skater in the world. The thing was, watching him now wasn't much different. He always made it look so easy, like he was born on a board and didn't have to follow the laws of gravity. He glided up to rock on the coping and slid back down again to do the same thing on the other side. "Rock to fakie," I whispered to myself, remembering the term for coming down with the rear end of your board first. He rolled down and back up, doing a frontside 180 as if it was nothing more than breathing. Then he popped back up beside me, and the Tyler guy dropped in. My dad quirked his eyebrows and smiled at me, waiting for me to be impressed.

I was.

But I turned away and studied the scuffed and peeling paint of the deck, the tracks of all the previous skate sessions embedded in the wood. Did he think I'd be so grateful to him for taking my turn that I'd forget everything else? Suddenly the thrill of watching these guys skate vanished. I was glad when a voice from below called out that the tacos were ready.

I followed Arlo to the big table where Gus was helping a woman in a tank top and shorts with reddish-brown hair put out different bottles of hot sauce. When she smiled at me, I could see a big red, orange, and black tattoo of a bird over her collarbone and up part of her neck. Arlo's name ran down her arm in cursive lettering that ended with a small red heart. "You must be Daphne! I'm Rusty," she said. "Come fix yourself a plate!"

I thanked her and took the paper plate she handed me and made my way around the table, loading up my tortillas with beans and meat and salsa.

At the end of the taco assembly line, Gus was doling out beers from a big red cooler. I watched my dad closely. The blue can Gus tossed him was the same kind of bubbly water Mom drank. "You want one?" my dad asked. I nodded, and he handed it to me. I kept my eyes on him. When he took another water, the knot in my stomach loosened.

"Daphne, over here!" Arlo was off to the side, waving me over to a chair next to him. I glanced at my dad. He'd pulled up two chairs. His face fell, but he pasted on a smile and said, "Sure, go sit with Arlo."

I sat down next to Arlo and put my drink on the ground. I balanced my plate on my lap and bit into the taco. Arlo slid his eyes over to my dad and back to me, his eyebrows slightly raised.

"What?" I said. "Why are you looking at me like that?"

He shrugged. "I just thought—well, the way your dad was talking about you, I thought you were best buds or something."

I scowled. "Nope. We are definitely *not* best buds."

Arlo laughed. "Yeah. I got that. So what's up between you two?"

I shrugged. There was no way I could tell him why I wasn't thrilled about spending time with my dad. "I haven't seen him in a few years," I said. "We're just not that close."

"Same," Arlo nodded. "I only see my dad a couple times a year. He has a new family in Arizona." He frowned.

"Oh." Whatever I'd been holding tight inside relaxed a little. Arlo and I had a couple of things in common: single moms, dads who weren't around. I'd felt the same way when I first met Sam and we were both the new girls at school. It was a little thing to share, but it was important. We didn't have to explain everything to each other, and that was pretty nice.

Arlo and I ate our tacos for a while without talking. Then he said, "There's a skate park near here, did you know?"

A skate park? I put down my taco. The old, familiar

longing hit me in a rush, so hard and desperate my nails dug into my palms: I did want to skate. "No, I didn't know."

"I've got my filmmaking class most mornings, but I'm free in the afternoon," Arlo said. "If you want to check it out, let me know. Bonus: If we go skating together, my mom won't be able to make me help Gus work on his house." When I didn't say anything, he pressed. "So, you want to go?"

I took another bite of my taco and chewed, keeping my eyes on the paper plate in my lap. "Nah," I said finally, shaking my head. "I'm not really into skating."

4

It was about nine when we got back to my dad's. We both stood awkwardly in the living room. "So what do you usually do at night?" he asked. "After you eat dinner, I mean? At home."

"What do you mean?" I asked. "Like brush my teeth?"

He laughed. "No, I mean, like, what do you and your mom do when it's just the two of you hanging out?"

Seriously? As if he could do whatever we did and suddenly become Perfect Dad? Did he expect me to suggest movie nights? To curl up on the couch and eat popcorn with peanut M&M's and dissect the skills of the actors with *him*?

"I don't know," I said. "I'm kind of tired. I think I'll go to my room."

"Oh. Sure," he said. I saw that flash of disappointment in his eyes again, but I turned my back and went down the hall. It sure wasn't my fault he didn't know how to hang out with his daughter.

I leaned back against the big pillows on my bed and sighed. Finally, I could relax. Having a room with a door that closed was probably going to be the best thing about the time I had to spend here. The faint sound of the television floated down the hall, and an image appeared in my head of my dad sitting out there alone. Then of him stepping in so quickly at the bowl, rescuing me from my dread. I shook my head to erase the picture. He was taking his turn in the bowl, that was all.

My phone buzzed. A text from Mom! I picked it up, glad for the distraction.

> Hey Babygirl, I'm in the 🚕
> on the way to the hotel!
> We'll video chat later, but
> for now just checking in.
> How was your night?

My finger paused on my phone for a second before I tapped out a reply. Went to a dinner thing tonight with his friends. I didn't mention the skate bowl.

Nice! Any kids?

A boy my age, Arlo. He's OK.

A boy! How OK is he? 🖤🖤🖤?

No! 🙄 Not like that! How about you? Have you met people yet?

Aw, you just want to know about the secret lives of the ⭐⭐⭐

When your mom's a star, the rest of them don't seem that special 😳

😆 Not yet, but maybe someday!

I'd been on edge all day, careful about everything I said and did. It was nice to sink into the familiarity of joking around with Mom, even if she was ten thousand miles away. But then her next text wasn't a joke:

Hey, thanks for putting up
with your dad while I do
this. 😌 It's going to end up
being so good for both of
us 😁

My finger hovered over the phone. *But it's so hard to be with him,* I wanted to type. *I can't deal with that puppy dog way he looks at me! You said you'd try to get me out of here!* But I knew how important Mom's acting career was to her. She was nervous about her first big break. I wasn't going to stress her out by pushing her. Not yet, anyway.

At least I have my own room!

That's right. I heard his
parents helped him buy a
house. Must be nice.

I'd been thinking I'd text her a picture of my room, or maybe even a little video tour of it, but her text stopped me. Mom never came out and said it, but I was pretty sure Dad had never paid any child support. I didn't want to rub it in, when we'd never been able to afford our own place. While I was thinking of what else to say, another text popped up.

35

Babygirl, I'm exhausted. Gtg
so I can rest up before the
first table read! 😘 🥱

OK. Love you! 🖤 🖤 🖤

I turned off my phone.

I got up early the next morning, but not as early as my dad: I could already hear the shower going. Good. I was kind of hungry, but if I left now, I wouldn't have to talk to him. More importantly, he didn't have to know what I was about to do.

I pulled on some clothes, tiptoed into the living room, and found the board and helmet my dad had tried to push on me yesterday. I grabbed them and slipped out the front door.

A thin veil of fog gave the houses an air of mystery, so different from July in Southern California, where it was usually bright and sunny in the morning. I carried the board under my arm until I turned the corner at the end of the block. Glancing over my shoulder to make sure no one was around, I placed the skateboard on the sidewalk and strapped on the helmet.

I stared at the sparkles in the charcoal grip tape. Watching my dad's friends in the bowl last night had felt like coming home to a place I'd forgotten about. The sound of wheels rolling over the plywood, their trucks grinding the coping, engaged something in my brain; the *click-clack* of boards riding up and down the transition woke up my heart. It filled me with something I'd stuffed down for so long.

Keeping my left foot on the ground, I touched my right foot to the front bolts of the board, then immediately pulled it away, like the board would bite me or something.

I was overreacting.

I took a deep breath and stepped onto the board, right toe forward, left foot pressed onto the tail. I leaned from side to side, using my body weight to turn the board. Without warning, a memory crashed over me: standing on my own board for the first time, my dad's hands holding me steady while I found my balance. "You're goofy foot like me," he'd said, laughing when I worried that something was wrong. "Nah, it just means you put your right foot in front instead of your left. Lots of people do. Tony Hawk, for one." He'd been as excited as I was that we were finally skating together.

Anger flared inside me, and I hopped off. The last thing I wanted was to let my dad think we had anything in common. I grabbed the nose of the board, ready to forget the whole thing. But then I froze, the board pressed against my leg. Deciding not to skate didn't make me feel any better. It made me feel worse!

I dropped the wheels to the ground again. Why was I making such a big deal out of it? No one had to know about this but me.

I placed my right foot on the board and pushed off with my left foot. Just that simple movement made a smile tug at the corner of my mouth. I told myself to start off slow, but my body took over. It remembered everything: how to stretch my leg out long in front to make maximum use out of each push; how to unweight, lifting my upper body to ease the board over cracks on the sidewalk; and how to tic-tac by pressing down on the tail of the board to pivot the nose back and forth as I turned a corner. I pushed down a long block, the wheels thrumming under my feet as I bent my knees slightly to balance and glide. I hadn't skated since I was ten, but it all rushed back to me: not just how to do it, but how right it felt. How free.

Back then, skating had freed me from worrying

about my mom and moving around so much. Today, it worked the same magic: My anger fell away as I glided down the sidewalk. I didn't think about my mom sending me to Oakland, or my dad expecting everything to be fine between us. The world focused in tightly to hold just me and my board.

How could I have forgotten how much I loved this?

The streets were narrower here in Oakland, with big trees and front yards that were a tangle of flowers, not like my Glendale neighborhood, where people had iridescent green lawns or cactus gardens. I took it all in and forgot where I was headed, relishing how the cool morning air kissed my skin and smiling as the vibration of the wheels on the sidewalk tickled the soles of my feet.

But as I came down 16th Street, the soaring feeling crash-landed. My heart started thumping against my chest as heavily as the skateboards on the deck last night. Only instead of celebrating someone landing a trick, my heart was telling me to turn back.

I'd found the skate park.

I could see the ramps rising up behind the basketball court in front of me. An older guy dribbled a basketball and shot free throws, but no one else was around. I pushed my board over to the chain-link gate at the skate park entrance and stopped, looking the place over.

I saw a big bowl, stairs to fly over, railings to grind on, and walls to ride up. Every bit of concrete was covered with graffiti and the black marks of millions of wheels from thousands of boards rolling through. It was perfect.

I opened the gate and skated past the easy transitions and over to the bowl. Last night, just the idea of dropping in had set off a panic. Here in this skate park, though, anything seemed possible. The old chant started back up in my head: *Ollie, nollie, kickflip, shuvit. Backside, frontside, fakie, grind.* Being back on a board felt great, but I wanted to *do* things.

I wanted to drop in! But that was ridiculous. Wasn't it?

I stepped off my board and glanced all around to make double sure no one was watching. Then I picked up my board and ran up the sloping concrete to the top of the bowl. I walked to the center of the ridge and chewed my bottom lip. I carefully set the tail of my board over the coping, then pressed my left foot onto the tail so the board hovered in the air, my other foot still on the ledge of the bowl. If I pressed my right foot onto my board, I'd drop into the bowl.

I looked down, and memories filled my head: mean laughter, blood dripping down my knee, my arm bent in a way it wasn't supposed to bend. And my dad nowhere to be found.

I picked up my board and walked back down the concrete slope, away from the bowl.

Nothing had changed. I was still a complete failure.

5

Even when I was little I could tell it bugged Mom when I asked her when I was going to see Dad next. She wouldn't put him down exactly, but her voice would get this hard edge, and she'd say stuff like "Your dad hasn't bothered to let me know what he's doing lately." Always "your dad," as if he had nothing to do with her.

So I learned not to ask her about him and to hide the constant ache of missing him. The ache got worse the longer he stayed away, which would be for months sometimes. I couldn't tell Mom how I wondered if he'd forgotten about me or worse, if I'd done something to make him not want to see me. So I stayed on high alert, checking Mom's phone to see whether she'd talked to him lately, keeping an eye out for his ancient silver BMW when I walked home from school. He did that a few times, showed up as a special surprise. It was always like magic. The instant I saw him, all my doubts would vanish, and we'd pick up right where we'd left off. Dad would flash his dimple at me and say, "What do you feel like doing today, Daf?"

What we ended up doing most was going to skate parks. We'd watch other skaters for a while, and then Dad would find me a place to sit, somewhere out of the way of the skaters but where I could still see, and I'd watch him skate. He'd look over at me every so often and call, "You okay, Daf?" and I'd nod eagerly, proud of my dad the skater.

When he called me on my tenth birthday, it had been even longer than usual since I'd seen him in person—a whole year. Hearing from him was as exciting as the new cell phone Mom gave me. I took my phone into the kitchen so she couldn't listen to our conversation. I hated the way her lips got tight when I talked to him.

He asked me what I wanted for my birthday, and I said I wanted him to teach me how to ollie. "That's it?" he said, and laughed as if it was no big deal. I didn't remind him that the last two times we'd talked on the phone he'd said he would teach me some skate skills but never had. I just said yes, and he promised to meet me at the skate park the next Friday.

It was just after I'd started hanging out with Sam, so I told my mom I was going to Sam's house after school. I lied. Mom might have been okay with me going to the skate park with Dad, but I didn't want her to nag him about keeping me safe. What if it made him not want to come? Besides, the skate park was only a few blocks from school. I'd never gone by myself, but it was easy enough to get there.

On Friday, I stood at the entrance of the park, the sound of wheels sliding over the concrete filling my ears. Excitement spiraled in my chest, but it was kind of intimidating to go into the park on my own. Four sixth-grade boys who'd gone to my school the year before skated by and said "Hey!" Seeing people I knew gave me the courage to skate the perimeter and check the place out.

I imagined myself someday carving the different bowls, sailing over stairs, grinding on the rails. I passed by some old dudes—even older than Dad—in the kidney-shaped bowl. In the corner of the park, away from the bowls, were some tiny kids with their dad, a boy and a girl the exact same size—twins, I guessed. The dad held their hands and pulled them along while they balanced carefully. I was sure Dad would have done the same with me too if Mom had let him give me a board when I was that small, but she'd always said it was too dangerous.

I pushed my board out to the center of the park. No sign of Dad. I watched a group of older kids dominate the smaller bowl, three white boys with shaggy hair hanging over their faces and a Black kid with short locs. They all wore T-shirts with skate company logos and beat-up Vans. You could tell they were the kids who hung out at the skate park all day, every day. The locals, Dad would call them. They were the loudest group in the park, laughing when anyone fell down, whooping when someone landed a trick.

I pushed over to a snake run where I could pump over the mellow transition, enjoying the lift in my stomach as I flowed. When I'd asked Dad for skating tips the couple of times he'd called me since I got my board, he'd told me not to worry about tricks—it was way more important to get comfortable on my board first. I took him at his word and skated everywhere I could. I was proud of all the bruises and scratches I got from falling. Dad said getting banged up was part of being a skater, the more scars the better.

I kept stopping to look around for Dad and pull out my new phone to see if I'd missed his call or text. I watched a guy ollie up onto a rail and into a 50-50 grind. I smiled, imagining myself up on that rail after Dad taught me how to ollie.

The ollie was the basis of all the more hard-core tricks. No matter how many times I watched skaters do it, I was always amazed at the way riders could leap into the air and the board would stay right there with their feet, like the skateboard was a part of their body. I couldn't wait to capture that magic for myself. With Dad helping me, I'd learn it easily.

I figured since Dad wasn't there yet, I might as well skate. I had to get up some nerve to ride over to the sixth graders, but they folded me right into their group. We took turns pushing up a low bank and barreling down the other side as fast as possible, laughing whenever we wiped out, then getting up and starting again. It was so fun I almost forgot why I was at the park to begin with, but when one of the sixth graders said, "I'm out," the others started peeling away too. One of them said I should hang out and skate with them again sometime, and I grinned and told them for sure I would. I loved the way our boards bonded us, made us part of something together.

After the last one left, the sun was on its way down. Where was Dad? I stood in the middle of the park, looking around. The dad with the little kids was trying to talk them into leaving. Almost everyone else had left too. I pulled my phone out again. It was almost six thirty. I'd been there three hours. No missed calls showed up on my screen.

Crash! Something slammed into my side, and I stumbled but caught myself. It was one of the locals. On the sidelines his friends were whooping. "Snaked by a little girl!" one called.

"Sorry!" I said, embarrassed that I'd broken the cardinal rule of skating and gotten in someone's way. I should have known not to stand in one place in the middle of the park. I rubbed my ribs where he'd rammed into me and waited for him to apologize, but the guy just popped his board up into his hand and curled his lip. "Better stick to the baby park," he sneered. "This part's for the real skaters."

He skated back toward his friends, who were all watching, laughing at me as if I had no right to be there.

Dad always talked about the community of skating, how skaters watched out for each other, so long as you weren't a poser just pretending to be a skater because it was cool. If you tried your best, Dad said, no one would judge you. I threw my board to the ground and hopped on, pushing away in anger. Those guys were definitely judging me!

"I *am* a real skater," I said out loud. I skated over the bank again to prove it to myself, but it wasn't fun anymore. I wished the sixth graders hadn't left. Their absence made me feel the other absence even more. I bit my lip, fighting the tears that prickled my eyes. Was Dad not coming?

I pulled out my phone again. I was new at texting, so I kept it short: Dad, where are you?

No. I sounded mad at him. I deleted and tried again.

I'm at the park! Are you on your way?

No. He *said* he'd come. He was on his way, I was sure of it. He was probably driving, so he couldn't text. I erased *Are you on your way?* and added a skateboard emoji and a heart. There. I was just letting him know I was here so he wouldn't have to worry.

I imagined him rushing into the skate park, frantic because he'd gotten stuck in traffic, looking all around and catching sight of me right as I executed a perfect ollie.

Well, of course I couldn't ollie yet, but maybe I could do something else that would impress him.

I skated over to the bowl with the rude skater boy and his friends and climbed to the top. One of them was skating in the bowl. As he rolled out, I tried to make my voice strong and confident. "Can I go?"

The guy who'd crashed into me shrugged and said, "I'm not in it anymore, am I?"

But a guy with a beanie like mine was a little nicer. "This is pretty steep," he said. "Have you ever dropped in before?"

I shrugged, unwilling to tell him the truth.

"Go ahead," the guy who crashed into me muttered. "This should be good."

I stood there, my back feet on the tail of my board on the edge of the bowl, the nose hovering in the air. I had never dropped in, but I'd seen it done plenty of times. I'd even watched some videos on how to do it, preparing myself for when Dad would have time to teach me. I knew you were supposed to lean in with your shoulder, but then what? My eyes flicked down to the bottom. Beanie guy was right: It was a long way down. I clenched my teeth, trying to gather my courage.

"Any time now, little girl," one of the locals mocked. I could see the scorn on the boys' faces, but I was more worried about Dad. Had something bad happened to him?

I had a wild thought: *If I do this, everything will be okay. Dad will be fine, and he'll be here any minute.* I sucked in a breath, placed my right foot onto the front of my board, and leaned forward. I was dropping in! I felt the slap of my front wheels against the wall.

For a split second I thought I'd done it. Then my board sprang out from under me, and I fell backward. The concrete met my body with a stinging smack, and pain sliced through my arm. "Ow ow ow ow," someone was saying. They were crying too, and then I realized both sounds were coming from me. My arm was on fire, and all I could do was lie there at the bottom of the bowl, even though I knew those guys would get mad at me for getting in their way again. Blood dripped from a gash in my knee.

Dimly I heard steps running down the bowl, and someone—beanie guy, I thought—asking if I was okay. I just sat there crying until I heard a man's voice, and my heart lifted. "Dad?" I sobbed. But when I looked up, it wasn't *my* dad; it was the twins' dad, saying we should call an ambulance. Mom would have a fit. "No," I moaned, cradling my left arm with my right hand as I rolled myself up. I knew ambulances were expensive. "I'll call my mom." With my good hand I reached into my back pocket. The screen on my new phone was cracked. "Mom?" I said, and then I started crying and couldn't stop.

The twins' dad took my phone and talked to Mom.

By the time she got there, all the locals had disappeared.

Mom didn't say anything to me. She thanked the twins' dad and got me into the car and took me to the emergency room. She waited until after the cast was on my broken arm and my knee was cleaned up and bandaged. Then she lit into me.

"Daphne, you lied to me! Why were you at that park all by yourself?" She pressed her hand to her forehead. "I hate to think about what could have happened if you didn't have your phone with you."

"Dad was going to meet me there," I muttered miserably.

Mom sucked in a breath and didn't say anything for a minute. Then she let out a long sigh. "Daphne, I don't know why your dad told you he'd come see you. There was no way he could have. When he called on your birthday, he was calling from his parents' place in the Bay Area. Your grandparents are trying to help him get his act together." At my confused look, she explained, "To stop drinking."

My eyes widened. Mom had told me a long time ago about Dad's problem, that when he started drinking alcohol, he didn't know when to stop. She'd said it made him do stupid things, even though "stupid" was a word she didn't let me use. But now he was trying to quit, and that's why he didn't come to the skate park. "That's . . . good, right?" I was still disappointed, but if it was so he could get better, maybe it was worth it.

"No, Babygirl." Her voice was soft as she took my good hand into both of hers. "I don't think it's going so well. He should know not to tell you he's going to come and see you without checking with me first. That tells me he's still drinking."

"Oh." I pulled my hand out of hers. Tears started dripping down my cheeks. "Okay."

"Your dad will be fine." Mom sighed. "Somehow he always manages to be just fine. But, Babygirl, you can't worry me like that. I need to know I can trust you when you say you're going somewhere. So here's the deal: You're grounded for the next week, and no skating for two weeks after the cast comes off." I could tell she was waiting for me to protest, but I nodded and wiped my eyes with the sleeve of my T-shirt.

The worst part? The part that made me feel extra, extra clueless later? I kept texting and calling Dad. Even though he never answered my text from the skate park, I thought Mom had it wrong. I was still willing to hear his excuse for not showing up. I even held back on telling him about my broken arm in a text because I wanted to hear his voice over the phone, telling me that now I had real skater street cred!

But he didn't text, and he never called.

I'd loved the names of skate tricks. For as far back as I could remember, whenever Dad and I saw each other, we'd spend some time leaning our heads over his phone to watch skate videos together. He'd trace his finger over the screen and tell me the name of each trick as the skaters landed them. One name that stuck with me was the disaster. You could do it frontside or backside, but either way it involved rolling up a ramp, doing a 180 ollie and straddling your board over the coping before you rolled back down again. The disaster part was that if you weren't careful, your back trucks could get hung up on the coping and you could pitch forward off your board. One time we watched a video of a guy doing a disaster that actually broke his board in half! Dad and I both let out the same dismayed "ohhh-hhh!" and then turned to each other and laughed.

I didn't break my board at the skate park, but something else broke, and it wasn't just my arm. I'd always thought of our love of skating as an unbreakable bond, but Dad made it clear he didn't see it that way. In my head, that day became the Skate Park Disaster and Dad became "my dad," as if he had nothing much to do with me. Because he didn't.

When my grounding was over and Mom said it was okay for me to skate again, I glared at my board leaning against the wall, taunting me. I couldn't stand the sight of it. I buried it in the back of our closet.

I haven't touched it since.

A few months after the cast came off, Mom said that my dad was going to start calling me once a month.

"It's okay, Mom," I told her. "I don't need him to do that." I knew she was mad at him over the Skate Park Disaster. It was nice of her to try to get him to make it up to me. But it wasn't going to work.

"Honey," she said, "it's not a choice. I think it'll be good for both of you to have regular contact with each other."

I stared at her in disbelief. Why was she changing her attitude about my dad now? "What about his drinking and stuff?"

"Well, he's been sober for two months," Mom said. "Let's see what happens. He won't put you in any danger just by talking on the phone! But if he starts slurring or sounding funny in any way, you hand the phone right back to me, okay?"

"Fine." I shrugged. I didn't bother telling her that hearing from my dad once a month because she was making him call wasn't going to change how I felt about him. It just proved he didn't care enough about me to make an effort on his own.

On that first call I waited for him to say something about why he never showed up at the skate park, but he never even mentioned it. Instead, he told me how much he missed me.

I wasn't foolish enough to believe that anymore, not without some proof. "So when are you coming to see me?" I challenged.

He was quiet for so long that I thought we'd been

disconnected. Then he mumbled, "Uh…it's a little complicated." He paused, but I wasn't going to make it easy for him by filling in the silence. He finally came out and said it: "I don't think that's going to work right now, Daf."

I could have asked why. I could have told him how much it hurt that he didn't show up at the skate park. I could have told him that part of me still hoped he'd teach me to ollie someday even though I wasn't skating anymore. But revealing all that stuff to him felt dangerous somehow. So I didn't say anything, and he just asked me boring questions like "What have you been up to?" and "How's school?"

When I told Sam how much I hated talking to him, it was right around the time her own parents split up. That was when we started the Cold Fish. We'd make our voices as dull and dead as possible to show how little we cared about our parents' problems. "Not up to much," I practiced saying with absolutely no expression, and Sam would add, in a robotic voice, "School-is-okay." Then we'd burst into laughter.

But there was no laughter when I talked to my dad. The fun we used to have together was over. Now it was just him calling me because he had to and me waiting for the call to be over.

6

The first thing I did when I got home from skating was to carefully lean the board against the wall in the living room and place the helmet on the floor beside it, exactly where I'd found them. Then I made my way to the kitchen.

My dad was sitting at the little table drinking coffee, but he stood up quickly when I came in. "Hey! There you are. I was kind of worried when you weren't here. Maybe text me next time."

"Mhm," I said. Mom would have given me a lot more grief than that, but my dad obviously didn't know the rules of parenting, and I wasn't about to give him any tips. "Is there any cereal?"

"Right there." He pointed to the cupboard on the other side of the sink, and I crouched down to look. "Were you out skating?" he asked.

"No." I grabbed the box of Cheerios and stood up.

"Because you know there's a skate park not far from here, right?"

"Right." I had to open a couple of cupboard doors to find the bowls. I grabbed one and poured out some cereal.

"I can take you over there if you want."

I pulled the milk out of the fridge and glared at him, but he didn't get it. His eyes were wide with expectation, like he thought I would jump up and down with excitement at his offer.

I poured milk over the cereal and brought it to the table. "Nah. That's okay."

My dad leaned back in his chair. I'd never seen him in a tie before. He wore a dark blue blazer over a pale blue button-down shirt and dark pants, very different from the old T-shirt and faded jeans he'd worn yesterday. His hair was still a little damp from the shower.

"Got a job interview," he said, seeing me noticing.

"It was supposed to be later this week, but they called and asked if I could come in today. I didn't want to say no, so I'm going to have to leave you for a little while. You can chill here, or Gus said you can go over and hang out next door if you want. Arlo's supposed to be there soon. You two kind of hit it off, right?"

"I guess." I shrugged. "I'm fine on my own."

"Anyway, I shouldn't be too long." He put his coffee mug in the sink. "We're going to your grandparents' for dinner tonight, so make sure to be back by five o'clock, and let me know if you go next door."

"Okay."

He cleared his throat. "I better go. Have you seen my keys?"

"Uh, they're in your hand?"

"Oh, right!" He laughed. "I guess I'm nervous. Well, see you later." He bustled around, grabbing his backpack off the back of the chair and slinging it over his shoulder.

It reminded me of Mom and all the times I'd helped her find her keys and purse before she left for an audition. It was my job to remind her to breathe and say she was going to do great. If it was Mom going out right now, I would have thrown my arms around her in a giant hug, breathed in the smell of her perfume, and told her I knew she'd knock them dead.

My dad patted his pockets, looking for something.

I just watched.

"Oh, here it is!" He picked his phone up off the counter and tucked it into a pocket of his backpack. Then he glanced over his shoulder at me as he walked out of the kitchen. "See you tonight."

I lifted my hand in a silent wave.

After I finished my cereal, I wandered through the house. I could hear the muffled sound of hammering next door and birds chirping in the trees outside, but the only sound inside was the refrigerator buzzing. It was too quiet. I went back to my bedroom and pulled out my phone to check my world clock. It was 11:00 AM here, so 8:00 PM in Prague. Perfect. I pulled up Mom's number on my phone and selected VIDEO.

When her face appeared on my screen, I realized how much I really, really missed her. "Hi, Mom!" My voice cracked, and I tried to laugh it off, but she could tell I was trying not to cry.

"Hi, Babygirl! Look!" She pointed her phone away

from her and turned in a circle. Rolling hills of green grass and leafy trees filled my screen. "We're in the countryside outside of Prague. Isn't it gorgeous?"

I knew she was trying to distract me, but it worked. I swallowed my tears. "It's really pretty. What have you been doing?"

I settled back against my pillows as Mom told me all about meeting the other actors and getting ready for her first scene tomorrow. I tried to pretend she was just coming home from a regular day at a job and wasn't thousands of miles away.

"But how about you, Babygirl?" she said after a while. "What have you been up to?"

I shrugged. I didn't feel like talking about myself. "It's pretty boring around here."

"Well, you know what I always say!"

I did. It was Mom's stock reply, and we said it at the same time: "A bored person is a boring person." We both laughed. "It's true!" she insisted. "You need to get out there and make something happen. What about your dad though? Everything okay with him?"

"I guess," I mumbled.

"But he's taking care of you, right?" Her voice had that edge it got when she talked about him.

"Yeah. He's on a job interview right now." I didn't want to talk about my dad either. "Mom, when am I going to come and see you?"

But someone was talking in the background on her end, and she turned her face away from me.

"Mom!" I insisted. "What about me visiting?"

She looked back, but I could tell she was distracted. "We'll see. Wait till I get a chance to suss everything out here." Someone's hand appeared on her shoulder, and a voice said, "We're leaving in five minutes! You ready?" Mom smiled and nodded at whoever it was, then turned back to me. "I'm sorry, honey, but I really need to go! Love you!"

I told her I loved her too, and we hung up.

A few minutes later, my phone buzzed with a text.

Sorry I had to hang up so quickly. Rachel invited me to dinner with some of the others tonight. We won't have much time to socialize after this. Starting tomorrow it'll be work, work, work!

Rachel was the starring actress and was also one of the producers of the movie. It was huge that she'd taken

Mom under her wing. If she invited Mom to do something, Mom was definitely going to do it.

> Tell Rachel you miss your daughter and you need her to visit.

Haha. Love you Babygirl, so so much.

> Have fun, love you!

We typed our usual slew of heart emojis, and that was it. I was alone again.

I drifted into the living room feeling more restless than ever and flopped down onto the saggy couch. I saw some framed pictures on the bookshelf behind the TV and got up to look. Without my dad around, I could snoop a little. I passed over two grayish pictures of old-timey people and stopped at a familiar one: me as a newborn baby, all swaddled up in a blanket, just my head and a shock of dark hair showing. Mom had a giant version of that photo that she hung up wherever we lived. I'd never thought about my dad having the same picture.

I picked up a small stack of loose photos. The first

was of a skater, board midair, soaring over a flight of stone steps, arms flung out to his sides like he was flying. He *was* flying. It looked amazing. I could tell it was my dad: He had the same scruffy beard and black beanie pulled over shoulder-length brown hair that I remembered from my childhood. The next photo was three skaters sitting on a low concrete wall. I didn't know who the first guy was, but I recognized a younger Gus. Grinning next to him was my dad, holding his board on his lap with one hand and the neck of a bottle in the other. A whiskey bottle. I let out a slow breath. Was he drunk in this picture?

One time when I was about seven and he came to visit me, Mom pushed him back out the door saying, "No way. Not when you're like this." That was the first time she'd told me about his drinking problem. She gave me a big speech about how if I ever saw him drinking anything or if I thought he was acting funny when he was with me, I had to call her right away. It scared me at the time, but it had faded from my mind pretty quickly. Back then, when my dad came to hang out with me, pretty much everything faded except for the fact that we were together.

I flipped through the rest of the snapshots quickly—

my dad wasn't in any of them—but I stopped at the final photo. It was me and my dad. It must have been taken on my ninth birthday, because I was hugging my new skateboard to my chest. I was leaning against my dad's leg and looking up at him. He had his arm over my shoulder and was looking down at me. We had matching one-dimpled grins on our faces.

The picture brought the day rushing back to me, how my dad had handed me a big black plastic garbage bag with a huge red bow stuck to the top. I'd fallen instantly in love with that board. "It's a Nora Vasconcellos Welcome deck," he'd told me as I stroked the bright blue three-eyed teddy bear graphic on the bottom of the board. "Spitfire wheels, Ace trucks."

I rubbed my cheeks now, remembering how they'd hurt from all my smiling that day. Dad had handed me a helmet and kneepads too, even though he never wore them himself. "Your mom would kill me if you got hurt," he said. And then we skated together.

I'd wobbled and fallen off a bunch, but he'd made me feel like a natural. By the end of that day, I was able to push off and glide a little bit on my own. "Next time I'll teach you to ollie," he'd said.

There had been no next time.

A sound outside brought me back to the present. Out the front window I saw Arlo skating up to Gus's door. I glanced down at the picture of me and my dad, shaking my head at the worshipful expression on my face. If the Skate Park Disaster was a dark cloud in my memories, then this day had been a blaze of golden sunlight.

They were both torture to think about.

I slapped the photo onto the bookcase, facedown. Mom was right. I needed to make something happen.

7

I grabbed the skateboard and helmet, mimicking Mom in my head: "A bored person is a boring person." I put the helmet on, marched across my dad's dried-up yard to Gus's, and knocked on the door. I held the board against my leg and strummed my fingers on the deck. I hoped Arlo wouldn't remind me that last night I'd told him I wasn't into skating.

Arlo opened the door. He was wearing gray sweatpants and another big black T-shirt, this one with a picture of Bart Simpson on a skateboard. He stared at me, then his eyes fell on the board in my hand. "Oh, you want to skate? Hold on, let me tell Gus, and I'll grab mine."

He disappeared for a second and came back wearing a helmet. "Ready?" When I nodded, he jumped on his board. I took off after him, smiling at how effortless it had been to make something happen. I hadn't even said a word yet.

I followed behind, glad he knew the neighborhood so I didn't have to worry about where we were going, soaking up the *kkkssshh* of our wheels barreling down the sidewalk, grinning when a little girl watched me zoom by, her eyes huge.

When Arlo slowed to a stop, it took me a minute to realize where we were: the entrance to the skate park. It wasn't empty anymore. The playground was filled with little kids, the basketball court had a game going, and about twelve people were skating, all boys.

I turned to Arlo. "I can't ride here."

Arlo squinted in confusion. "I thought you wanted to skate?"

I cupped my left elbow in my right hand and rubbed it. "Not here." My chest got so tight that I couldn't inhale, and I couldn't take my eyes off the boys skating up and over the small rises in the middle of the park. Two of them almost collided, and they laughed as they stumbled off their boards. I stepped back and slammed the tail of my board with my foot so it popped up into my hand. "I have to go."

"Hold on, hold on!" Arlo said, lifting both his hands. "We don't have to stay here. I know another place. This way." He pushed off past the skate park without checking to see if I was following. I laid my board back down and pushed off behind him, the breeze soothing my hot cheeks, my breath gradually steadying. I knew my reaction was strange. I was glad Arlo didn't ask me about it. I kept my eyes on the ground, lifting them only high enough to see Arlo's legs. When he kick turned around a corner, I did the same. Kick turning isn't really a trick, it's just something you have to do if you want to travel on your board. I'd been so proud when I'd taught myself how to do it by watching other people. I'd wanted so badly to tell my dad about it.

Arlo stopped. We were at a school. It had that sad, deserted air that schools always have in the summer. A sign out front said LAST DAY OF CLASS: JUNE 6! Not a soul was in sight. Arlo motioned for me to follow, and we walked down a little alley behind the school and up to a long chain-link fence.

"Is this your school?" I asked.

"Was," he said. "Before middle school." We walked

along the fence until we came to a waist-high gap. "Some kids cut it out so they could bring their bikes back here," Arlo said, ducking through the hole. "I don't know why the school people haven't closed it up yet, but it's not a bad place to skate."

I ducked under, and we cut across the playground, passing a grassy field to get to the big parking lot. "Ready?" Arlo laid his board on its side and did a twisting kick thing so that he somehow ended up on top of it.

"Wait. What was that?" I asked.

He grinned. "That? A wraparound. Just something I picked up. Pretty cool, right?"

"Can you do it again?" The words popped out of my mouth before I had time to think. Arlo had a way of making it easy to ask about stuff I didn't know.

"Sure," he said. "I'll put it in slo-mo for you." Extra slowly he bent down to pick up his skateboard and laid it on its side.

"Cool." I laughed. "I think I got that part."

He grinned again. "I can't help it. I think cinematically." Then he got serious and showed me the move slowly, narrating along. "You put your heel in front of the back wheel, like so. Then you kick your foot back in a circle so the board wraps around your back foot, and then you have to jump off your front foot as it lands and you get on top." He jumped and landed on his board while I studied his feet. So cool. How did he made it look so effortless?

"Your turn."

"What?"

"Don't you want to try it?"

I did. Of course, I did! But I stepped back, gripping the edge of my board tightly. "Oh. Nah. I don't do tricks." Before he could ask any questions, I threw my board down and rode off. After a minute I could hear him behind me.

We skated back and forth across the lot, bombing down the slight hill as fast as we could. When we both stopped to catch our breath, Arlo pointed toward the school. "There's some speed bumps over there."

"Let's go," I said. If I could unweight over sidewalk cracks, I could go over these low speed bumps too. I took the first one slow, leaning back on the tail of my board and tipping the nose into a mini manual, which is like popping a wheelie on your bike. I went over it once and tried again, taking the speed bump a little faster, and then even faster. Soon enough Arlo and I were rocketing over them side by side, whooping as our boards *ka-thunk*ed over the bumps. We turned around to do it again, but this time as I popped over the bump my board flew out from under my feet. I landed right on my butt. "Ow!" Pain rocketed up from my tailbone.

When Arlo noticed I'd fallen, he skated over. I slowly pushed myself to my feet. "You hurt your elbow?" He pointed to the way I was rubbing it.

"No." I dropped my arm. "I'm fine." But I wasn't. My mood had come crashing down as hard as my butt. I bent over to pick up my board, moving stiffly from the pain. "I think I'm done."

"Hmm. Maybe we should get boba before we go back," Arlo said. "Boba always makes everything better."

I cast a sharp glance at him. Could he tell what a bad mood I was in? But he stood there, a slight smile on his face, looking at me hopefully. I shrugged. Boba did sound good. "Sure."

Ten minutes later we slid into the hard plastic booths at a Quickly and punched our straws through our drinks— Thai milk tea for me and lychee for Arlo. He took off his helmet and pressed his drink against his sweaty forehead. I pulled on my straw and relished the cool milky sweetness of the tea sliding down my throat.

"So why didn't you want to go to the skate park?"

There it was, the question I had been dreading. I shrugged, keeping my eyes focused on the pale orange of my drink. "I don't know any tricks."

"So? You can just ride around. Besides, not knowing any tricks *now* doesn't mean you won't ever know any."

"I just don't want to, okay?" I snapped. "And I don't want to talk about it either." I poked at the bobas in the bottom of my cup with my straw, mad at Arlo for asking, mad at the way those old feelings kept coming back: the humiliation of the Skate Park Disaster, the anger at my dad, and snaking underneath everything, my longing to go to the skate park despite it all.

"Okay! Sorry!" He held his hands up. "I will never, ever bring up skate parks again." The corner of his mouth lifted, so I knew he wasn't offended.

"Thanks," I said. I liked the way Arlo made things seem like not a big deal.

We tossed our cups into the trash and skated home.

At the front door, I toed my board up into my hands. It had been fun skating with Arlo. I was thinking maybe I could put the board in my room this time, when the door flew open.

"Where were you?" My dad stood in the doorway, his jaw tight.

"Out with Arlo, skating."

He frowned down at my board, like he didn't understand what he was seeing. Then he shook his head. "I asked you to tell me where you were."

That was so unfair. "But I was with Arlo. You literally told me to hang out with him!"

"I also told you to let me know where you were! I was really worried! Why didn't you answer your phone? I called you a million times. Arlo wasn't answering either."

How was I supposed to know he was going to call? "Sorry. My phone's dead, and Arlo's ringer was off."

"That's not good enough!" he shouted.

I flinched and backed away from him, the board banging against my leg.

His eyes widened in horror. "Sorry, sorry!" He opened the door wider. "Come inside," he said in a calmer voice. "Sorry I yelled."

I bit my lip and went inside.

My dad ran his hands through his hair. "It's just... I'm responsible for you. If anything happened to you, what would I have done? How would I have found you? I was getting ready to call hospitals!"

"Sorry," I muttered. "I got back on time anyway."

He reached out as if he was going to . . . I don't know, hug me? Grab my hand? Whatever it was, he dropped his hand. "So I guess I should have been more clear about the rules. I'm just so happy you're here and—"

"Okay, okay," I interrupted. I didn't want to hear him tell me again how great it was that I was visiting. As far as I was concerned, his enthusiasm was too little, too late. "Do I have time to shower before we go?"

"No. I mean, yes, you have time, but wait a minute." He whooshed out a breath. "Look, Daf. I know we haven't done this before. I know I need a little practice." He flashed his dimple at me, and I answered with a stony stare. The dimple disappeared. "Okay. Ground rules. I need you to call or text me if you're going anywhere, if you're going to be late, if you need a ride. I have to know where you are at all times. Got it?"

Seriously? *He* was giving me a hard time for not letting him know where *I* was? But I just muttered, "Got it." Mom had drilled into me how important it was for her to always know where I was and what I was doing. I knew that was a parent thing.

I just didn't know my dad knew it too.

8

Mom says it's being an only child that makes me so good at hanging out with grown-ups. For a while she was the only one of her friends with a kid, so she carted me around everywhere. I thought of her friends as my friends too.

But I wasn't used to *old* people. Mom's dad died before I was born, and I'd never met her mother. They weren't close. Whenever Mom talked to her on the phone, she had to go for an extra-long run afterward "to get that voice out of my head," she said.

So in the car on the way to my grandparents' house in Berkeley, I worried: What if they didn't like me?

What if they really did think sending me fifty dollars on my birthday was all they needed to do? I thought of the Christmas cards they sent me every year, always with a photo of themselves in red-and-green sweaters, their dog with a Santa hat on her head, but I couldn't really remember their faces. Would I even recognize them?

I pulled out my phone. My dad hadn't said anything about staying off my phone while I was in the car with him, and I wasn't going to let him know that Mom would never allow it.

Dinner with my grandparents tonight, I texted Mom.

Don't believe anything they
say about me 😏

???

Let's just say they know I
don't appreciate their noses
in my life, so they're not my
biggest fans. But they love
YOU, honey. Don't worry! 😚

K. Better go, almost there.

I turned off my phone without giving her a chance to reply. She wasn't helping my nervousness.

A few minutes later, my dad hummed under his breath and parked the car. I guessed he didn't mind visiting his parents. Mom's comments still echoed in my head though. Why didn't they like her? And how was she so sure they'd like me?

My dad turned off the engine, but he just sat there, drumming his thumbs on the steering wheel. I reached for the door.

"Daf, wait."

I sank back in my seat.

"My mom's really excited you're visiting. Dad too of course, but especially her. She's been calling me every day asking me what you like to eat, if you're a vegetarian, if you like chocolate." Abruptly he stopped drumming. "Look." He turned to face me. "You've made it pretty clear you're not thrilled to be here, but I have to ask you to do something. I need you to rise above your feelings about me and be nice to her. To both of them. Please."

I picked at the car seat where it was coming apart. It wasn't that I thought my dad wouldn't notice how I felt, but it was awkward hearing him say it out loud. And he didn't even know I planned to leave as soon as Mom cleared it with her movie people. "Okay," I said.

We got out of the car and headed toward the house: a big brown two-story with a garden full of flowers and a brick path to the front door. All down the block trees lined the sidewalk, so tall they created a canopy over the street, and the neighboring houses were equally big and pretty. Were my grandparents rich?

"Mom! Dad! We're here!" My dad walked right in without knocking. I guess that made sense: It was his parents' house. I followed slowly, looking around. The house was fancy in a woodsy sort of way. Wooden floors, furniture with wood slats on the sides, a big wooden table with a huge vase of purple flowers. I looked at my scuffed-up Vans, my faded jeans, and my red thrift store T-shirt. But my dad was wearing a T-shirt and jeans too. He would have told me if I should have dressed up, right? I watched him disappear into the kitchen.

"Where is she?" a woman's voice said.

I got an impression of straight, chin-length gray hair and a tall, angular shape like my dad's before I was engulfed in a hug. "Daphne! I'm Grandma Kate." It wasn't anything like what I imagined a grandma's hug would be—soft and squishy, smelling of flowery perfume. Grandma Kate smelled of soap, and her bony shoulder poked into my neck. But I didn't mind. I wrapped my arms around her.

She let go just enough to grasp me by the shoulders and look me up and down. She was wearing jeans too, so she probably wasn't judging my clothes. It was more like she was hungry and trying to eat me up with her eyes. It made me a little nervous. Then her eyes got sparkly, and she laughed and said, "Oh, look at me, getting all misty. But it's so, *so* good to see you. Now, why isn't your grandpa here?" She turned away and sniffed, then called over her shoulder. "Joseph, go get your dad. He's out back."

"In a minute!" My dad disappeared up the stairs.

Grandma Kate made a little *tsk* and pulled me by the hand into the kitchen. I was glad she was taking charge. I couldn't seem to get any words out. "Can I get you anything to drink? We've got some of that sparkling water your dad likes, or some lovely organic apple juice, or maybe some nice cold tap water?" She was still watching me in that eager way, which made it even harder to say anything. "How about the juice? I think you'll like it," she said after I didn't answer. When she turned to open the fridge, I let out a small sigh of relief. I looked around.

The kitchen was fancy too, big and open with an island that held a glass bowl filled with a green salad dotted with little red tomatoes. Sunshine streamed in through the windows, bright and cheerful. A sliding glass door led out to the backyard. A big tree in the corner shaded half of it, so it took me a minute to notice a man bent over a barbecue. My grandpa? Then I saw the brown dog lounging on the back deck, and my tongue finally untied itself. "Is that Lady?" I recognized her from the Christmas cards.

She handed me a glass of juice and nodded. "That's Lady. Getting a little lazy in her old age, but I'm sure she'd love to say hello. You can say hi to your Grandpa Jim at the same time. Wait." She reached into a ceramic jar on the counter and handed me a bone-shaped dog biscuit. "Lady will especially love it if you give her this." I stared at the biscuit. I'd always wanted a dog, but whenever I begged Mom for one, she said it was too hard to find places to live that allowed pets. I liked the idea of saying hi to Lady, but I wasn't really sure how to do it.

I slid the glass door open and took a half step toward the dog, who lifted her eyes but didn't seem particularly interested until I extended the biscuit.

She lumbered to her feet and sniffled at my fingers. I stretched them out flat and squeezed my eyes shut. What if she bit me by accident? I felt a wetness on my hands and heard crunching, but it was the biscuit, not my bones. Lady licked her mouth and eyed me with approval. I kept my hand out, and she licked until she got every last crumb. I got brave enough to slide my hand on top of her head and scratch it. Lady moved in next to me, closed her eyes, and leaned against my legs.

"That means she likes you." My grandpa was watching us. "Of course, she likes just about everyone, but it's still pretty nice to have her lean on you, isn't it? Like she trusts you."

I nodded. It was exactly like that. My grandpa strode over and extended a hand. "It's good to see you again, Daphne. I'm Grandpa Jim." I took his hand and squeezed lightly, noticing the calluses on it. He shook my hand firmly, but I was relieved he didn't stare at me like my grandma. He just went back to the barbecue and started flipping the meat over. I held as still as I possibly could so Lady wouldn't move and studied my grandpa. He looked more relaxed than he did in the Christmas pictures. He stood straight and tall and wore a T-shirt and jeans. He turned around and said,

"Would you mind telling your grandma I'm ready for a platter?"

I nodded and slowly pulled one of my Vans out from under Lady. She gave a little doggy sigh and lay down again, and I went back inside. "Um, Grandma?" The word felt strange coming out of my mouth. "He's ready for a platter." She lifted a giant blue plate from the kitchen island and handed it to me. "Here you go, dear." Dear? I smiled. It sounded like such a grandma thing to say.

I took the platter to my grandpa, who told me to hold it for him while he piled it with grilled vegetables: eggplant, peppers, green onions, and a giant mushroom. "Take that in and get me the other platter, will you? Meat's done, which means it's time to eat!" I nodded, but I still hadn't said anything to him. Why was being around my grandparents making me so bashful?

I took the platter in, and before I could ask, my grandma handed me another one that was big and round with flowers painted all over it. "We've got it down to a science," she said. "It's not our first barbecue, you know."

I presented the plate to my grandpa, and he carefully laid the meat on it, one piece at a time, big slabs of brown steak, black on the edges, pink in the middle. Lady stayed very close, her eyes pinned on the plate, waiting for me to drop something. After my grandpa emptied the grill, he lifted the plate from my hands and announced, "Dinnertime!"

We walked inside together, and Grandma Kate called upstairs, "Joseph! What are you doing up there? Come on down!"

My dad came down carrying a crumpled brown paper bag. "Just digging around for some stuff for Daphne."

I eyed the bag. What could be in there? But I turned away before he could notice my interest.

"Daphne, you sit here, by your grandpa," Grandma Kate was saying. "I'll sit over here, and Joseph, you're there, across from Daphne." We took our places, and the plates started moving around the table.

"So!" my grandma said to me after we'd all served ourselves. "You getting settled in? That's quite a nice room your dad fixed up for you, isn't it?"

"Mm-hmm." I popped a piece of steak into my mouth so she wouldn't expect me to say more. I wanted to be polite to her, but not if it meant saying how great my dad was. The steak distracted me. It practically melted in my mouth. Mom didn't eat red meat, so I hardly ever did either. "This is really good," I told my grandpa.

He nodded with a little smile, like it was no surprise to him. "How's your mom doing?" he asked. "Heard she got a part in a movie. Always did think she had potential in the acting business."

"You did?"

Grandma smiled. "I remember one time we were babysitting you when you were about four. That commercial she was in—remember Joseph? Some cleaning product?" My dad nodded. "Well, it came on the television, and you made me back it up so we could watch it over and over. You couldn't get enough of seeing your mama on TV!"

"You babysat me?"

My grandparents both froze and caught each other's eyes across the table. "Yes, of course," my grandma said finally. "I guess you'd have been too young to remember."

I could feel my cheeks growing warm. The memories of my dad swooping in and out of my life were so clear in my mind. I wished I remembered my grandparents babysitting me too.

"Well." My dad cleared his throat. "You guys didn't

come down to see us that much after Daf was, what, about five?" He cleared his throat again. "When Edy and I stopped getting along so well."

Eden, I wanted to tell him. She hates it when you call her Edy. But I was too interested in the conversation to make a point of it. Why did they stop getting along?

My grandpa turned to my dad. "As I recall, you made it pretty difficult for us to come and see you."

My dad looked down at his plate. "Yeah. I know. Sorry."

Grandma's eyes slid back and forth between Grandpa and my dad, her eyebrows drawn together. "It wasn't all his fault," Grandma said. "Eden could have let us—"

"Mom," my dad said. "Let's not go there."

Grandma sat there for a second, her mouth still open. Then she turned to me and said brightly, "I remember picking you up from that apartment in Burbank, when you were staying with your mom's friend Sheri for a while. I'd take you to a park right near there and push you in the swings for hours. You never got tired of them."

I squinted, trying desperately to recall anything about it. I got a little flash of reaching up to hold hands with someone walking me across a big sandpit to the swing set. "Was there one of those curly slides too? Right by the swings?" Grandma nodded. "I think I remember!" We smiled at each other.

I went back to my steak, my mind rewinding the conversation. I had to ask. "How did he make it difficult?" I looked from my grandpa to my grandma. One of them had to answer. "To see him," I added, when neither responded.

"Oh, you know." Grandma Kate sipped her water and raised her eyebrows at me.

"I was drinking too much," my dad said. "Mom, you can talk about it, it's okay. It's part of recovery to admit you screwed up."

"That's right, you were a mess," Grandpa agreed. He turned to me. "Never could pin him down either. Always off on those trips."

"What trips?" I asked.

"Skate trips." My dad smiled. "When I first moved to Southern California, I was trying real hard to get sponsored, you know? It was right about the time I met your mom. She was taking acting classes, and I was trying to go pro."

"You both had such big dreams," Grandma reminisced.

My dad nodded and turned back to me. "I was on

flow for a couple of companies—you know, getting free gear—and I knew a few guys who actually made money from skating. They let me tag along on a couple skate tours. Then Gus came down to visit me for a few weeks. He didn't care about the competitions I was trying to win. He was always more into just having fun—bombing down hills and skating anything he could find to skate."

"It's so nice that Gus and you live close to each other again," Grandma put in. "He always did stick by you."

"True," my dad agreed. "Anyway, Gus said we should go on a 'tour' too, but something totally different from those official ones. No contests, no kissing up to sponsors. The goal was to hit as many different skate parks as possible. We camped in between, some beautiful places. Hot springs, hiking trails. We had such a great time, we made sure to take a skate trip every time Gus came down to see me. Got a bunch of friends into it too." He let out a sigh. "Be nice to do something like that again at some point. Sober, this time. You ever been camping, Daf?"

I stared at him, trying to reconcile this picture of

his life when he lived in L.A. with what I knew of him back then, which had never been enough. I couldn't even imagine him and Mom talking nicely to each other, much less sharing their dreams. And were those tours the reason there'd been months and months when I didn't see him? "Nope," I said. "I've never been camping."

"Yeah, I guess not. Edy never did like sleeping on the ground much."

Mom went camping with you? I wanted to ask. Instead, I said, "Eden. She doesn't like to be called Edy."

My dad laughed. "That's right. Eden sounds more like an actor name, doesn't it?"

"Well, I'm just glad she got such a good part," Grandma said. "And I'm even more happy that we get to see you, Daphne! In fact, I told your dad you could stay with us—"

"Mom," my dad said. "Stop."

"I'm just letting her know—"

"She's staying with me. We talked about this."

My eyes darted between my grandma and my dad. Were they fighting? Over me?

Then Grandma Kate smiled as if my dad hadn't

even said anything. "Well, I know your dad wants to spend as much time as he can with you, but I insist on getting lots of grandma-granddaughter time in too! I was thinking I could take you into San Francisco. We can go to Pier 39, Fisherman's Wharf, ride on the cable cars, whatever you want."

"Mom, that's overpriced tourist stuff," my dad said. "Daphne doesn't care about all that."

I glared at him. I didn't know anything about those places, but my dad sure didn't get to decide what I cared about. Besides, now that I'd met them again, I wanted to spend as much time as I could with my grandparents before I took off for Prague. "Actually, I'd love to do that. It sounds like a lot of fun!" I said to my grandma.

She smiled at me, and I grinned back and glanced at my dad out of the corner of my eye. To my disappointment, his dimple was flashing too.

9

So what'd you think of your grandparents?" my dad asked as he unlocked the door when we got home. "Not too bad, huh?"

"I liked them." The truth slipped out. My dad's face brightened like he'd just heard the best news ever, and I wished I hadn't said anything. I was definitely glad my grandparents were back in my life, but I had to make sure my dad knew I wasn't suddenly okay being here with him.

"I'm going to bed," I said.

It worked; the brightness vanished. "It's still early, I thought we could—" He broke off. "Sure, of course." I was halfway down the hall when he called out, "Daf?" I turned. "Catch." I instinctively reached up and caught the crumpled brown paper bag. "Just some old swag I had. Anything you want in there is yours."

I looked at the bag. "Okay."

"Go ahead and decorate that board if you want. I know you've been riding it."

I frowned at him, ready to deny it, but he'd already turned away. I tossed the bag onto the bed. I sat down and pulled out my phone, hunching over the screen so my hair fell like a curtain between me and the bag. Sam had emailed me, a long note about her camp and what they'd done the first couple of days. Her sleepaway summer camp had "limited screen time," so no phones were allowed, only a once-a-week trip to their computer lab. Every summer we had to get used to communicating through email, but it was always hard at first because we were used to seeing each other just about every day.

When Sam and I met, Mom was waitressing at night and doing acting stuff as much as she could during the day. I ended up going to Sam's house a lot after school, and I felt instantly at ease with her two cute younger brothers, who'd follow us everywhere if we let them. On the weekends, Sam came over. Even though our place was so much smaller than hers, she thought Mom was glamorous and loved our routine of eating take-home restaurant food from wherever Mom was working and watching movies together on her big bed. Afterward, we gave ourselves manicures and talked about the movies, critiquing the actors.

But just because we liked each other's families didn't mean we didn't know about the problems. I was the one Sam cried to when her parents split up, and she was the only person who knew how much I worried about what would happen if my mom never realized her dream of making it big someday. If Sam was here, I'd tell her everything that had happened since I stepped off the plane.

But I didn't really feel like writing it all in an email right now.

I sighed. It was no use pretending I wasn't curious. I dumped the contents of the bag onto the bed. A pile of stickers and a couple of T-shirts fell out.

The two shirts were both black and both huge. One had the logo for the skate magazine *Thrasher* across the front. The other had a face inside a red flame with a toothy evil grin, the Spitfire logo, the brand of wheels on my skateboard at home. The stickers were mostly Spitfire too, in a rainbow of colors, but another had a red monster with yellow horns. I picked it up, trying to decide whether the monster was scary or funny. Both, maybe. I ran my fingers over the stickers' glossy smoothness.

No.

I shoved everything back into the bag. If my dad had given me this stuff when I was a kid, I would have been dumb enough to think it meant something. But I knew better now. I crumpled up the bag to toss it across the room, but my arm froze in midair. The board I'd been riding was leaning against the wall. My dad must have slipped it in here earlier.

I grabbed it and lay back on my pillow, hugging the board to my chest, the grip tape scratching my skin. I suddenly remembered how I actually slept with my own board for a while, as if it was a cuddly stuffed animal.

There was something about tonight's visit to my grandparents that I couldn't get out of my head. Back when I cared about my dad, before the Skate Park Disaster, I'd learned to recognize the tight look on Mom's face that meant I shouldn't ask when I would see him next or why he hadn't visited lately. Even when she announced she was shipping me up here, she didn't talk about him.

But tonight at dinner, my grandparents and my dad

did something my mom never did: They talked about the past.

Mom had told me early on about my dad being an alcoholic, but I wondered about so many things, stuff she wouldn't get into. Like, what made him not be able to control his drinking? And the big question: Why didn't I ever get to see him enough? It couldn't *all* be because of drinking alcohol. Could it? Before the disaster I used to make excuses for him. After, I figured that if he really wanted to be in my life, he'd have found a way. Tonight's dinner conversation made me sure of that. He managed to go on all those skating trips—why didn't he manage to see me too?

Too bad the one person who had all the answers was the last person I wanted to ask.

I scooched into a sitting position and flipped the board upside down, running my fingers over the shallow scratches there. I hit the back wheels and watched them spin, thinking. Maybe my dad wasn't the only person I could ask. Maybe Grandma Kate would tell me some things.

I dug through the paper bag till I found the red flame sticker. I wondered whether my dad had gotten it on one of those tours he'd talked about. I peeled the backing off and stuck it to the bottom of the board.

I smoothed my hand over it. It looked good.

But it didn't mean anything.

The next afternoon, Arlo was the one who knocked on my door. "Skate sesh?" he asked. He wore a black backpack and held his board in his hand.

He was so casual about it, like this was now the thing we did together all the time. "Yep," I said. "Just a sec."

I was on my way out, board in hand, when I saw my dad at the kitchen table on his computer, muttering at the screen. He seemed upset. I hesitated, running a finger around the edges of the new sticker on my board. Then I scowled. Not my problem. "I'm going skating with Arlo," I said.

He looked up at my face and then down at the board. I braced myself for the too-happy look that would surely appear on his face, but his eyes flicked back to his laptop. "Okay," he said. "Text me if you're—"

"I know. I'll text you if I'm going to be late."

"Or if you go anywhere else," he called after me, but I was already closing the door behind me. I followed Arlo as he headed down the sidewalk, grinning to myself as I bumped down a curb. I wished I could ollie up onto the other side like Arlo did, but I lifted my face to the afternoon breeze as we cruised along and focused on my feet and my board and the ground underneath. I didn't pay much attention to where we were going. When I finally glanced around to get my bearings, I realized we were on the same block as the skate park.

"Don't worry," Arlo called as he drew near the entrance. "I won't try to make you skate here."

Behind him, I slowed and stopped, standing with one foot on my board and one on the ground. I shielded my eyes and watched the skaters who filled the park. Arlo skated back. "What, now you want to go in?"

I shook my head, but I couldn't take my eyes off this one guy doing a boardslide down a stair railing. He made it look like no effort at all.

Arlo watched me watching. "Want to hang out and watch?"

I wrinkled my nose. "Won't it be weird if we're not skating?"

"Who cares?" But when Arlo saw my frown, he said, "No. It's fine to watch." He slid his backpack off and pulled out his camera. "Maybe I can get some good shots in."

We slowly skated through the park. Skaters zoomed back and forth in front of us, and the wonderful sound of wheels whirring and clacking filled my ears. Arlo nudged me, and we climbed to the top of the bowl, my eyes darting around trying to take it all in: A boy, probably high school age, skating the half-pipe, grinding the coping, and rock 'n' rolling. An older guy with a mustache kick-flipping onto a railing. Another guy sailing over a flight of stairs and landing in a crouch on his board.

Down in the bowl, a board flew out from under a skater's feet. I flinched as the board rolled right into the path of another guy. "Board!" a bunch of people called, and the guy managed to swerve around it without crashing. The skater whose board it was shouted "Sorry!" He grabbed it and skated back as if it didn't even matter.

How did people not run away in shame when they messed up like that? "Did you see that?" I turned to Arlo, but he was fiddling with some settings on his camera.

He pointed the camera at the guy who'd sailed over the stairs. Now the skater was heading up a transition so steep that it was really more of a wall. A big graffiti eyeball stared out from the center. He skated straight up and around the eye, his feet glued to his board. "Whoa!" I exclaimed. "That was *so* cool!"

"Hey, that's Isaiah!" Arlo lowered his camera. "Let's go say hi."

He was right: It was the guy my dad said was so good. I followed Arlo, who was already calling out and jogging over. Isaiah fist-bumped Arlo and smiled at me. "Hey," he said, nodding at the board in my hand, "I didn't know you skated."

"Sort of." I shrugged.

"She skates," Arlo said. I frowned at him. "What? You do!"

"Don't worry about it," Isaiah said. "If you're even a fraction as fearless as your dad, you're better than most. You two hanging around? Come skate with my crew over there." He pointed over to some guys clustered at the top of a ramp.

I shook my head, but I couldn't get any words out. Isaiah seemed really cool. I wanted him to think I was cool too, but panic was tightening my chest. I had to get out of there. *Now.*

"Actually, we were just leaving," Arlo said. "I have to talk to Daphne about a film I'm working on."

"See you at the next Silver Bowl Sesh, then," Isaiah said. He hopped onto his board and skated over to his buddies.

Arlo and I headed toward a picnic table over on the grass. I took big gulps of air to calm myself down.

"Thanks," I muttered to Arlo. I sat down on the bench that faced the skate park. There were too many trees for it to be a clear view, but I could see skaters every now and then as they landed their tricks.

"For what?" Arlo said, shucking off his backpack and pulling out a notebook.

"For saying we were leaving." I stared down at the table. It was all carved up with people's initials and swear words and funny little drawings.

Arlo glanced at me. "Yeah, no worries. You made it pretty clear you didn't want to skate there. But actually"—he paged through the notebook—"I really do have to talk to you about a film. I'm taking this class over the summer, you know?"

I nodded. "You said."

"We're starting to work on our final project, a three-minute finished film, edited and everything. At the end we're going to do this film festival, where we each show what we did." He put his hand over a page in the notebook. The tips of his ears were turning red, and he wouldn't look at me. I got ready to be encouraging, even if it was a silly idea. "One of my friends wanted me to work with him and do a classic quest story with wizards and things, all using LEGOs."

Ah. "Wow. LEGOs *and* wizards?" That was pretty embarrassing.

"I know. Taking nerd to a new level, right?"

I laughed. I liked the way Arlo could make fun of himself.

"The thing is," he continued, "I used to be really into LEGOs. I have a lot of them. But stop motion is my friend's thing. These days I'm more into live action."

"Uh-huh." What was he getting at?

"So here's my new idea." He slid his notebook over to me and pointed at the little squares with stick figures drawn in pencil. I traced my finger over a line that sloped upward and out of the frame.

"Is that a skate ramp?" I asked. Arlo nodded. "Nice. A skater movie would be cool."

"Yes, but our teacher, Mr. Lamont, is always saying our stories have to have a beginning, middle, and end—I can't just shoot a bunch of sick tricks by random skaters. So this"—Arlo tapped his finger on the stick figure on the page—"this is actually...you."

I slid the notebook back to him. "Very funny."

"I'm serious!" Arlo said, his voice rising in excitement. "I want to document your journey."

I laughed. "Where am I going?"

"You're the one who gave me the idea," Arlo said. "It was the way you started out kind of cautious yesterday, and next thing you know you were bombing over those speed bumps! Fearless!"

Arlo thought I was fearless? I bit back a smile. But it wasn't true. "Till I fell down," I reminded him.

"Exactly!" He nodded. "Skaters make videos of themselves all the time, but I need to tell a story. So look." He tapped the first row of pictures in his notebook. "What if we start with you doing the basics, just skating, you know? Then"—he tapped the second row of stick figures—"like yesterday, you might take a fall. But you'll keep going, and you'll start getting better, landing some tricks." Arlo started talking faster, getting more excited. "Then finally here's you totally shredding, blowing everyone away. See? Beginning, middle, end! What do you think?"

I stared down at the picnic table. *Ride or Die!* someone had written in black Sharpie, with a little cartoon of a skateboard under it with flames shooting out the back. "I don't know," I said, rubbing my elbow. But actually I did. There was no way I could do what he was asking. "I don't know any tricks, remember?"

"That's the beauty of it! You can learn some! Don't worry, I'll edit it so you get the gist of how much work you put into it, but the viewers won't have to sit through each painful try."

I bit my lip. Skating with Arlo yesterday had been fun, but he didn't get it. Being in a movie would be like announcing that I was a real skater. And I wasn't.

"Hey, what if we added some drama?" He pounded his notebook for emphasis. "Like, if we got some of those guys in on it." He gestured back in the direction of the skate park. "They could pretend to make fun of you. You know, 'girls can't do that,' stuff like that. And then you show them what you've got!"

"*No.*" My cheeks flamed. "That's a terrible idea! I can't be in a movie!" I slid off the bench and turned my back to him. I heard Arlo slap his notebook closed.

I gripped the tip of my board in my fingers and stared at the skate park, embarrassed at how I'd over-reacted. But I wasn't about to tell Arlo why.

"Hey, it's no problem," he said, finally breaking the silence. "I just thought—well, you obviously like to skate, and I like filming skaters. I thought it would be a good partnership, that's all."

I turned around. He played with his camera, awkward and tentative, like he was the one who'd done something wrong. So far, skating with Arlo was one of the best things about staying with my dad. I didn't want to blow him off. "You can't fool me," I said. "I know you're just trying to get out of building a bunch of LEGO sets."

He grinned. "How'd you guess?"

We both laughed, and the tension relaxed.

I hesitated. "I'm sorry. I'm sure your film will be cool whatever you decide to do. But I just can't. Besides, I'm probably not even going to be here all summer. My mom's asking her producers if I can visit her in Prague."

"Oh," Arlo said in surprise. He studied me, as if considering whether to ask more. But then he said, "What flavor boba you getting today?"

"Hmm. Maybe mango. You?"

He stuffed the notebook into his backpack. "Lychee all the way."

I grinned, relieved he let the movie thing go so easily.

We skated off toward the Quickly.

That night, I finally got around to answering Sam's email. Usually she was the one doing new stuff at camp while I was bored back home, but this time I could tell her all about skating with Arlo and seeing my grandparents. Then I tried to write about my dad and how strange it was to be with him. In person, Sam and I talked about everything, but I just couldn't explain it right in an email. I deleted the stuff about my dad and wondered whether I should tell her Arlo's idea.

It had been nagging at me all day. It was kind of flattering that he wanted to make me the center of his film project. But he'd said the point was that I'd learn a bunch of tricks. In the two days since I'd started skating again, my old craving to learn more had come back full force, but how was that going to happen? I could barely bring myself to step foot in that skate park. No. Being in his movie was definitely a bad idea. If I told Sam about it, she'd tell me to go for it. She and her brothers had dragged me to enough baseball games where Sam rooted for what she called the underdog that I knew she'd especially like Arlo's idea about me showing the skater boys what a girl could do.

No, I wouldn't mention Arlo's movie to her. I signed off:

> Still not sure when I'll be going to Prague.
> Soon, I hope! I'll keep you posted. Miss you!
> xox

10

The next day, Grandma Kate took me to Fisherman's Wharf. She admitted that my dad was right and that no native San Franciscan would do this stuff, but we had fun anyway. We were watching a bunch of sea lions lounging around on the docks when a familiar *krsshhh* sound made me turn my head. Sure enough, two skaters were heading toward us. I stared.

They were both girls.

They wove through all the people easily, the short locs on the girl in front bouncing as she ollied onto a bench and landed a perfect kickflip as she came down. The girl with a blond faux-hawk behind her tipped into a nose manual, laughing as her friend tic-tacked ahead. I didn't take my eyes off them until they disappeared into the crowd of people.

"Your dad knows a woman who runs a summer day camp for girl skateboarders, you know."

I looked at Grandma Kate, startled. For a second I'd forgotten she was even there.

"We could see about signing you up for it. Would you like that?"

I felt a 360 aerial lifting in my stomach. A skateboard camp? That was all girls? Then the 360 came crashing down, a total fail. I lowered my chin. "No, thanks."

"Fine." She shrugged. "Should we get some ice cream before we head back?"

"Definitely." I nodded, glad she didn't push it.

But when Grandma Kate handed me my chocolate chocolate chip, she said, "You know, just because you're not getting along with your dad doesn't mean you can't do something he likes."

I stared at her in surprise. How did she do that? It was like she knew exactly how I'd felt the other morning when I almost didn't skate. I licked my ice-cream cone as we started walking again. Grandma was pretty smart. Maybe now was the time to ask her some of those questions I had. "So." I cleared my throat. "What was my dad like when he was my age?" It wasn't exactly what I wanted to know, but I couldn't just launch right into the hard questions.

"Your dad?" She licked her ice cream, smiling a little. "He was kind of a sensitive boy."

"Sensitive? What do you mean?"

"Here." Grandma Kate handed me a napkin. Ice cream was dripping down my hand. She waited till I cleaned it up. "Joseph had sort of a rough time finding his place when he was younger, you know? Then, just when he was about your age, we found out some kids had been bullying him."

"My dad?" I tried to imagine him getting picked on. I couldn't. "Why?"

"Why do kids ever do stuff like that?" Grandma shrugged. "Maybe they'd been bullied themselves, or they were scared of someone different from them. Anyway, your grandpa and I didn't even realize what was happening until the school called to tell us he'd been cutting class. We sat him down to talk about it, and he told us everything. He said he left school so he could get some peace. Know where he went?"

I shook my head. "Where?"

"Come on, take a guess."

"Ohhhh." I smiled. "The skate park?"

Grandma nodded. "He said watching the skaters made him feel better."

"He didn't go there to skate?"

"No, he didn't even have a skateboard."

My dad without a skateboard? That was almost harder to imagine than him getting bullied. "So what happened? Did you and Grandpa punish him for cutting school?"

"Your grandpa thought we should."

"That's what *my* mom would have done," I commented. Mom always went on and on about how important school was and how she was going to make sure I got the college education she never had.

"Even if you were being bullied?" Grandma asked, raising her eyebrows.

I thought about it. "Well, she'd go to the principal and make a big fuss about that, and *then* she'd ground me."

"That sounds about right," Grandma agreed. "Your mom can be very fierce, especially when it comes to you."

I narrowed my eyes at her. Was she putting my mom down? But she had a smile on her face, so I didn't think so. Besides, it was true. Mom did have that fierce side. "So, wait," I said, crunching into the cone. "You never said if you punished him or not."

"Well, we made a deal with him. See, he *begged* us for a skateboard."

"And?"

"And we said we would get him one if he stopped cutting school and kept up his grades. And he had to promise to tell us if anyone bothered him again."

"Did it work?" I asked.

"Yes." Grandma nodded and dabbed at her mouth with her napkin. "We were glad he stayed in school, of course. But the best thing about getting him that skateboard was that it gave him more confidence. He found some good friends too. Gus was one of them."

We were almost to the garage where we'd parked the car. I knew this was my chance to find out what made my dad abandon me, but I was stuck on the image of my dad as a nervous kid, learning to skateboard and realizing it was where he belonged. This time, I could really picture it.

It reminded me of me.

Grandma dropped me back at my dad's house, and I headed to the kitchen to get a glass of water. "Oh." I stopped in the doorway when I saw my dad sitting at the table, his hands in his lap, staring into space.

He looked up. "Oh, hi."

I filled a glass with water and drank it down, waiting for him to quiz me about my day in San Francisco, but instead he said, "Gus and Rusty invited us over for a barbecue. You want to go?"

"Okay," I said, surprised he was giving me an option. I leaned my back against the sink. There was something off about him, the way he was kind of hunched over, staring at nothing. "Is there anything we should do?" I asked. He lifted his eyes to look at me. "When Mom's friends have barbecues, we always make cookies or something to bring," I explained.

"Oh!" He nodded. "Thanks for reminding me. I said I'd bring a salad." He pushed himself away from the table and opened the refrigerator, pulling out vegetables. He grabbed a big wooden bowl and a cutting board and started slicing a red pepper, sliding the seeds out of the center with one easy motion of his knife.

"I didn't get the job I interviewed for the other day," he told me. "And the interview I went to this morning didn't even say wait and see—they told me right off I don't have enough experience."

"Oh." So that was what was off. "What kind of job are you trying to get?" I asked.

He shrugged. "Some kind of entry-level position at a tech company. I took a coding certification course last year. They told me I'd find something right away, but it's tough when you haven't held down a steady job in a while." He lifted the cutting board and slid the pepper slices into the bowl, then started slicing another one.

I'd seen Mom plenty of times after she got a call from her agent telling her the casting directors had decided to go with someone else. When that happened, it was my job to make her feel better. I'd tell her that there was another, better part waiting for her or that the people who rejected her would be sorry they ever said no to her.

I wasn't ready to be there like that for my dad. But I couldn't get the story Grandma told me out of my head. Watching his shoulders droop over the cutting board made it easy to see him as a lonely kid, watching people skate before he even had his own board. I put my water glass in the sink and grabbed one of the cucumbers. "Is there another knife?" I asked.

"In that drawer," he said, pointing. I didn't look at him while I got busy slicing.

"If you can do the tomatoes too, I'll get started on the dressing."

"Okay," I said. We didn't say another word as we finished making the salad.

But somehow it felt okay.

I found Arlo sitting at the table in the backyard. I sat down and grabbed a handful of tortilla chips from a big red bowl in front of him. "No one's skating?" I asked.

"Nah," Arlo said. "This is a neighborhood party. Gus says the point is to show everyone that even though he has a noisy skate bowl in his backyard, he's still a nice guy."

I looked around. People filled the backyard, grown-ups chatting, a couple of little kids running through the plants. Rusty and Gus were stationed at the grill, Rusty laughing and waving a brush covered with sauce in the air. I watched as Gus grabbed her hand and wrapped his other arm around her to draw her close.

They stopped laughing and stared into each other's eyes. They didn't kiss or anything, but it was almost more personal. I looked away, embarrassed.

"Does your mom ever have boyfriends?" Arlo asked. He was watching them too.

"Not really," I said. "Her friends try to fix her up sometimes."

I remembered the last date Mom went on. When she got home, she'd let out a big sigh of relief and said, "I only have room in my life for two passions: acting and you, Babygirl." No way was I telling Arlo that. I glanced over at Gus and Rusty again, who'd gone back to working together at the grill.

"Gus asked us to move in with him," Arlo said.

"Wow. Congratulations." I couldn't read his expression, but it was definitely not enthusiasm. "Or...not?"

"I guess," he said slowly. "I mean, sure. I like Gus fine." He looked at his mom again. "I just don't want to move in if we're not going to stick around."

"Why wouldn't you stick around? Gus must really like your mom if he asked you to move in with him."

"Yeah. Seemed like Salvador really liked us too." Arlo popped a chip into his mouth. At the question on my face he said, "The last guy. And with Dylan, and the guy before that too." Arlo squinted. "Harris? No, wait, Harlan. But it never sticks. I think my mom gets... kind of pushy."

I wasn't sure what to say. Arlo acted like it was all a big joke that his mom dated so many guys, but I was pretty sure he didn't think it was that funny. "So you don't think it'll stick with Gus?" I asked.

Arlo shrugged. "I wouldn't count on it. And my mom after a breakup? Not a pretty sight."

"Oh. Right." I understood that. "Like my mom when she doesn't get a part. I always have to comfort her."

"Yeah? What do you do?"

I thought back to the last audition she'd had before the movie, for a sitcom pilot that was supposed to be a sure thing. She was friends with the director, and he'd told her she'd done great. "I make her green tea and hand her Kleenex while she cries."

"That actually sounds familiar," Arlo said. "What else?"

I wrinkled my nose. "Sometimes I rub her feet."

"Gross." Arlo laughed. "At least I've never had to do that!"

Then I remembered something. "My grandparents said Gus has stuck by my dad for a long time. Maybe he'll stick by your mom too."

"Maybe." Arlo took another chip, but he just stared at it.

"Look," I said, wanting to make him feel better. "You wouldn't believe how many times I've had to tell my mom the perfect part is right around the corner. For some reason she always believes me, even though there's no way I could know what part she'll get!"

Arlo nodded. "My mom's always asking me what I think of guys." He rolled his eyes. "I keep telling her I have no idea and I don't care, but she still asks."

I laughed. "But the thing is, for my mom it turned out the perfect part *was* right around the corner. So who knows? Maybe the perfect guy is too, for your mom. Maybe it's Gus."

"That doesn't really make any sense." Arlo popped the chip into his mouth with a crunch. "But he is making chicken mole tonight because I mentioned I missed my abuela's cooking."

"Really? That's pretty sweet," I said.

"Yeah," Arlo agreed. He looked over at my dad, who was talking to a couple I didn't know. "So how's it going with your dad anyway? You guys getting along any better?"

"I don't know." I thought about chopping vegetables with him earlier, but I couldn't explain how that was different from before. "It's just weird."

"How's he feel about you going to see your mom in Prague?"

I grabbed a chip and spent a lot of time getting just the right amount of salsa onto it. "He doesn't know about it," I muttered finally.

Arlo blinked. "Wow. That'll be a fun talk."

"Exactly." I nodded. "That's why I'm avoiding it."

We both laughed, and then Gus announced the food was ready. We ate in a big circle with our plates on our laps. The grown-ups' conversation bounced from joking around to serious stuff like world politics and back to joking again. It was kind of nice, but underneath it all I had this itchy, restless feeling in my brain. I kept glancing over at the ridge of the bowl. It called to me. Why though? It wasn't like I could skate it. I couldn't even drop in.

We stayed at Gus's till after the sun went down, and then my dad said he wanted to get home so he could get an early start tomorrow and get some more résumés out before he went in for another interview. Everyone knew about his job search and wished him luck.

The stars were beginning to twinkle as we walked to our door. I rubbed my bare arms. It had been warm earlier, but I was cold now. My dad glanced over at me. "That's the only thing I miss about L.A., those warm nights. No matter how hot it is here during the day, you're always going to get cold at night."

He unlocked the front door and motioned me in ahead of him. "Actually, that's not true. The main thing I miss about L.A. is getting to see you."

I froze in the middle of the living room. He'd mumbled it toward my back, like by now he'd lost all hope that I'd say anything nice back to him. Which was a good thing because it was his own fault if he missed me.

But something stopped me from heading straight to my room, a combination of Grandma's story about my dad, the defeated way he'd told me his interviews hadn't gone well, and the words he'd just said. Since I'd arrived he'd mentioned a couple of times how happy he was to see me, but that didn't mean anything. That was just what he was supposed to say.

But the way he just now said he missed me? It was different somehow.

I turned around, then stood there, watching him sort through the mail he'd grabbed as he walked in, tossing things into different piles on the table by the door. It was true he didn't deserve my pity. But who knew how much longer I would be here? Mom might call tomorrow and tell me she got my Prague tickets. I didn't want to spend whatever time I had left here watching my dad and his friends in the bowl. I didn't want to only watch people at the skate park.

I wanted to be part of it.

"Um," I said.

My dad stopped. "Daf? Is something wrong?"

I shook my head. "I just…" I swallowed. "I mean, I was wondering…" He was looking at me with wide eyes, like he was sure I was going to say something terrible. Maybe I should leave it at that. Turn around, go to my room, and never let him know what I was about to say. But my feet were rooted to the floor, and before I could stop myself, the words rushed out of my mouth: "Could you teach me some skating tricks?"

He dropped the mail on the table and straightened up slowly, like a kid learning to balance on a board for the first time. "Sure," he said after a minute. "I could definitely do that."

"Okaygreatthanks," I said. I swung around and hurried down the hall to my bedroom without turning back.

"Good night, Daf," he called.

I didn't answer. I closed my bedroom door and leaned against it. Why was my heart pounding so hard? Was I nervous that I wouldn't be able to do what I'd been wanting to do since I first held my own skateboard in my hands? Was I excited that I might really learn all the skating tricks I'd dreamed of mastering? Was I afraid that now I'd asked my dad for something he'd let me down again?

Nervous? Yes. Excited? Yes. Afraid?

Petrified.

11

When I walked into the kitchen the next morning, my dad was leaning on the counter, sipping coffee. "Good morning!" he said cheerfully.

I lowered my eyebrows at him. "Morning." Just because I'd asked him to help me didn't mean we were best friends now. "Another interview?" He was wearing his button-down shirt and tie and blazer again, and his hair was still a little damp from his shower.

He nodded. "Sort of. My coding class instructor is going to introduce me to a couple people who might be able to help me. I'll be gone awhile, but Gus and

Rusty will be around. Check in with them if you go anywhere, okay? Tell them what you're up to."

"Okay."

"Arlo told me to tell you to come and help him paint his room, but it's up to you."

"Okay."

"We're still on for a skate sesh when I get home, right?"

"Mmhm." I rummaged in the cupboard for some cereal, hiding my face behind the door. I wasn't going to let him know it was the first thought that passed through my brain when I woke up.

"Sorry to leave you alone so much. I just have to take these opportunities when they come up, you know?" I nodded. He added, "I mean, I could call my mom again if you'd rather—"

"It's fine," I said. I wasn't going to admit that I worried if I went somewhere with Grandma, we might not get home in time for my skating lesson. "I'll hang out with Arlo."

"Good, good." My dad took one last gulp of coffee and put his cup in the sink.

I pulled the Cheerios out and poured some into a bowl. My dad started patting his pants pockets and looking all around in that panicked expression I was starting to recognize. "Over there," I said, waving the cereal box in the direction of his keys on the kitchen counter.

"Oh!" He picked them up and flashed me a grateful smile. "Thanks, Daf."

I turned back to my cereal. I didn't want him to get too excited about our skate lesson.

I didn't want *me* to get too excited.

Rusty greeted me with a huge smile when she opened the door. "Hey, Daphne! We were just wondering if you'd be coming over." She led me down the hall, saying, "I'm so glad you and Arlo have hit it off. He could use a friend close by. Changes, you know? Always a challenge." She stopped at a room where the door had been taken off. "Ta-da! Arlo's new room."

I recognized the scene: a huge tarp covering the floor, blue masking tape around the window and along the edges of the ceiling. If we were allowed, Mom and I repainted the walls every time we moved. We'd tried creamy yellows with bright red accents and delicate shades of beautiful blues. Once we'd had an artist friend of Mom's paint huge orange poppies all over our bedroom walls. But we'd never done plain old white. That's what Arlo was rolling onto the wall.

He turned at the sound of his mom's voice and shot her a look. Angry? Embarrassed? I couldn't tell for sure, but it was some kind of unhappy. "Daphne's here to help, Ar! Why don't you get her set up?" On the other side of the room Gus stood on a ladder, using a paintbrush to fill in the corners between the wall and the ceiling.

Arlo stopped painting and grabbed a bucket of paint. "There's another roller over there," he said. I picked it up and waited as he poured paint into a tray for me.

"It's looking great, boys!" Rusty said, still in the doorway.

Gus beamed down at her from the ladder. "It does look good, doesn't it? Nice and clean." He waved his paintbrush at me. "I actually got the idea from your dad, Daphne. He was adamant you get your own room so you'd know you belonged here. I want Arlo to feel the same way."

Rusty glowed. "Isn't he the greatest, Ar?"

Arlo rolled his eyes. "Yeah, Mom. The greatest." His

voice was so deadpan it reminded me of the Cold Fish. I giggled, but Rusty and Gus didn't notice. They were too busy smiling at each other.

I didn't know what Arlo was so worried about. It was obvious that Gus worshipped the ground Rusty walked on. "I still say you should sue that landlord of yours," Gus said, turning back to his painting. "Not that I want you to move back there, but it's discrimination, saying you have to move out because you have a kid."

"Nah," Rusty said. "I just want to forget about it and move on. Anyway, I'm off to work. See you guys later."

"Wait." Gus laid his paintbrush down on the little shelf on the ladder. "I need to grab something out of your car before you go." They both left.

"What do you want me to do?" I asked Arlo.

"We're on the second coat, so we just need to make sure it's even," he said, gesturing to the wall opposite the one he was painting.

I dragged the paint tray over and dipped the roller into it, flipping it from side to side to let the excess drip off the end. "You and your mom in a fight?" I asked as I started rolling paint onto the wall.

"Kind of. It's fine. Whatever."

"Ah. That clears it all up."

Arlo let out a short laugh, but he didn't explain. For a while there was only the sound of the rollers squishing paint over the wall. "So," I said finally. "White, huh? On every wall? Don't you find that a little...boring?"

"White's not boring. It's versatile."

"Versatile?" I snickered.

"Shut up. It makes the light good for filming. You know, in case I have to make a set in here. Which I might have to do, since my brilliant idea for a skate documentary isn't going to work out."

I dipped my roller again. I was glad I was facing away from Arlo. "I asked my dad to teach me some skating tricks."

"You did?" I heard his roller stop, but when I didn't turn around, he started painting again. "That's kind of a big deal, right?"

"Not really," I said. My words hung in the air. We both knew they weren't true. I bent to dip my roller again. "Well, maybe. But I'm trying not to think about it too much."

"Yeah, I know what you mean," Arlo said. He climbed up the ladder to take over painting the corners, and I kept rolling. We worked in silence. I'd always liked painting, and I got into the familiar rhythm: dipping the roller, the *squisssshhhh* of rolling paint onto the wall, then dipping again. I got so into it that it took me a while to realize Arlo was being extremely quiet. I played his last words over in my head. "Hey," I said. "What did you mean? What is it *you're* trying not to think about?" Was he that upset that I wouldn't let him do his skate documentary with me?

"Nothing," he mumbled. "Just . . . what I said before. Moving in here and all."

"Oh." I remembered what Gus had said. "Wait. Your landlord actually made you move out? I think Gus is right. He can't do that! My mom says landlords always think they can mess with single moms. Maybe you should fight him."

Arlo let out that same short laugh. "Nah. We're not going to do that." He climbed down the ladder to move it over to a new spot. "So what are you going to ask your dad to teach you first?"

"To ollie, of course."

"Too bad you couldn't get someone to document that. Like on film or something."

"Ha ha," I said.

"I want you to know I pulled all my LEGOs out of

the Goodwill donation bag, so now I'm depriving some kid of inheriting my carefully curated collection. That's on you."

I smiled. "You're just trying to pretend you were never a LEGO nerd."

He pointed to Darth Vader on his T-shirt. "You really think I'd bother to try to deny my heritage?" We both laughed.

But I could tell Arlo was worried about something.

12

The second I heard my dad's old Toyota pull up in front of the house, I told Arlo I had to go. I ran home and pretended not to be disappointed when my dad said he needed a minute to change his clothes.

I grabbed my board and waited outside for him. I was trying to stay calm, but my stomach was jumping around like it was doing the ollie I was hoping to learn. I told myself not to get my hopes up, but it was too late: They were already way, way up.

Next door, Arlo opened the front door and called out to me, "Let me know if you want me to come by and film."

"Yeah, right," I said, but I smiled and relaxed a little. A minute later my dad joined me outside.

"I hear you and Arlo have been skating at the school," he said. "That seems like a good place to start—less pressure than a skate park."

I squinted at him suspiciously. Did he somehow know I'd freaked out with Arlo at the skate park? But he was tugging on the brim of his hat, like he was as nervous as I was. "Okay, let's go to the school," I agreed.

I ran a few steps, dropped my board, and hopped on. My dad called out "Niiice!" behind me, and for some reason it made me mad. I pushed again, hard, trying to push away the memory of looking around for my dad at that skate park in L.A., no sign of him anywhere. But after about a block, skating started to work its magic, and my anger gave way to the solid feeling of my feet planted on my board and the thrum of my wheels on the sidewalk.

At a street corner we both tic-tacked in place as we waited for a car to go by. "You look good, Daf," my dad said. "I can tell you're comfortable on your board, so you've got a huge jump on learning tricks right there."

Wow. I couldn't let that go. "Yeah," I told him.

"That's what you told me last time we skated together." I hoped he got the point: *The only time we skated together. Three years ago, on my ninth birthday.* But I didn't wait to see. I took off and didn't stop till we got to the school. I hopped off my board and led the way to the hole in the fence and ducked through.

The hole was a little tight for my dad, but he managed to squeeze through. I watched him straighten and look around, and my fear came rushing back. What if I couldn't even come close to doing an ollie? Maybe this whole plan was silly.

My dad skated toward the grassy field.

"We're going to skate on the lawn?" I asked.

"Lesson number one: learn how to fall," he said, hopping off his board and popping it up into his hand.

I rolled my eyes at my dad. "I know how to fall. I fall all the time."

He pointed at me. "Exactly. Everyone falls. It's the picking yourself up again that counts. Those are the real skaters." He demonstrated a fake fall onto the grass, rolling onto his shoulder and back up again. "If you know how to fall so you don't get hurt, you've got it made. The trick is to roll when you land. Now you do it." We spent a while throwing ourselves onto the ground. It was kind of fun, covering my T-shirt in grass stains as I tucked in my arms and rolled.

"Okay, that's probably good for now," my dad said. "Let's do some skating."

We started skating around the asphalt as Arlo and I had. It was fun at first, but when I went over the speed bumps and my dad whooped, I hopped off my board, irritated. I wasn't some little kid. He didn't need to act like everything I did was totally awesome. I popped my board into my hand. "When can I learn how to ollie?" I asked.

"Let's do it!" my dad said. "Let's see what you got."

I stared at him. "What do you mean?"

"Well, you've been practicing, right? Let me see how you're doing it, and I'll tell you what you need to fix to make it work. It's probably the follow-through. You need to roll your front foot as you slide it forward—a lot of people miss that when they're first starting."

I rubbed my left elbow and looked down, my eyes feeling suddenly hot. "I've never really tried it," I mumbled.

"Never?" He tugged on the bill of his hat and squinted like he thought it was the strangest thing in the world. "Why not?"

That was too much, and I glared at him. His *not* teaching me to ollie had caused the whole Skate Park Disaster. I never talked about that day. Not even to Sam. "Can you just show me?" I didn't bother keeping the edge out of my voice.

My dad raised his eyebrows, but he nodded. "Sure." He walked along the asphalt, staring at the ground. I thought maybe he'd dropped something when he motioned me over. He pointed to a crack. "You want to start out with your back wheels wedged in here so your board won't slide out from under you. Now, watch me, but don't just admire my sick style." He stopped, but when I didn't laugh, he jammed his hat down on his head more tightly. "Anyway. Try to break it down into steps as you watch. Figure out what I'm doing."

"Okay."

My dad skated a little way away and ollied, over and over. Sometimes he'd change it up and do a nollie, which is an ollie that starts with the nose of the board instead of the tail, but it didn't matter which he did. Every time he popped into the air, my heart lifted right along with his board. I wanted to do that. I *needed* to do that. I pushed away my anger, squatted down on the ground, and glued my eyes to his feet.

My dad took off his cap to wipe the sweat off his face with the sleeve of his T-shirt then jammed it back onto his head. "So? You figure it out?"

I squinted in concentration, trying to replay what I'd just watched in slow motion in my head. "Well, you pressed down on the back of your board, and then you bent your knees before you went up."

"Good! What else?"

"Um, you jumped?" But that wasn't right. It was more than a jump. It was a magical way of making the board stick to the bottom of your feet as you lifted off the ground. "Oh! I know! It was like the back tilted up, and then you flattened your board out in the air."

"Right!" My dad grinned. He squatted next to me, holding his board in his hands. "See, it goes like this." He pressed the back of the board down so the front pointed up, then lifted the back up to the same level as the nose, and pushed it back down on the ground. "Basically it's three steps: the snap or pop, the slide, and the jump, each done at just the right moment in succession."

I nodded. "Got it." He made it look so easy. "Can I try?"

My dad laughed. "I was going to break it down into steps—"

134

"I just want to try," I insisted. I could feel it in my feet. I somehow knew it would come to me naturally. And wouldn't it be great if I could show my dad that I didn't really need him to teach me?

I wedged my back wheels into the crack my dad had found, then stepped onto my board and bent my knees like I'd seen him do. I pushed down on the back, I jumped and...pitched forward off my board, my arms flailing.

It was harder than it looked.

"That was actually pretty good," my dad said.

I glared at him again. I didn't want his pity praise.

"I'm serious. You've got a nice, loose stance. You look comfortable. But let's break it down. We'll start with the pop."

He had me stand on my board and push the tail down to the ground with my back leg so the nose rose into the air, my front leg resting on the front bolts. Then I was supposed to push down and let the board hit the ground. I fell off the first time, but after that I just kept rocking it up and down, up and down. I could almost imagine lifting the whole board up from here.

"Okay, now the slide," my dad said. He told me to go back to putting my foot on the tail, nose up, and then slide my foot up to the end of the board. "It's a matter of sliding your front foot forward on the board so hard you hear that *shsh* noise on the grip tape and you know you're going to eventually put a hole in your shoe," he said. At first it felt silly to stand there sliding my foot, but he was crouching down, so intent on watching my shoe leave marks on the grip tape that I got into it too, the *shsh* sending a pleasant chill down my back.

"Move back a little more, right here," my dad said, reaching out and adjusting my foot. I tried again. "Perfect!" My dad straightened out of his crouch. "Now we put it together and turn it into the jump that makes it an ollie. You ready?"

I nodded and couldn't bite back my grin. Sure, I'd failed that first attempt. But now that I had the steps down, I was sure I could do it. "Okay, here I go."

I snapped the tail down and...the board slid out from under me. I landed on my butt. I scrambled up and waited for my dad to tell me what I did wrong, but he kept his eyes on my feet and said, "One thing I left out: jump forward. It's like any trick. If you don't commit, it's not going to work. Falling forward means you're committing to the ollie. Try again."

So I tried again.

And again.

And still again.

No matter how many times I tried, I'd either do the pop right and fall off during the slide, or fall off before I even got to the slide. "You've definitely got the falls down. Aren't you glad we practiced?" my dad joked. I gritted my teeth. I couldn't laugh about this.

"Keep going," my dad said. "You've got the right idea." I didn't understand how he wasn't the least bit frustrated at watching me fail over and over, but his calm helped me get up and try again.

But I still couldn't do it.

"Aaaagh!" I screamed after the millionth try. I shoved my board away with my foot, and it rolled away from me. I sat down on the asphalt. "I can't do it!" I hugged my knees and let my hair fall over my face. "I just can't!" I hid behind the curtain of my hair.

I heard my dad's footsteps jogging away. Then he plopped onto the ground next to me and slid my board over so it tucked under my bent knees. "You can do it. I'm sure of it. You have the makings of a real skater."

I let my hands rest on either end of my board, feeling the comforting scratch of grip tape under my fingers. "Why? Because I'm your daughter?"

He laughed. "As far as I know it's not genetic. Nah. Skating's all about patience and determination and not being afraid to fall. You got that. If you keep at it, you're going to get there. There's just one problem: I can't be the only one who believes that." He tapped his finger on my knee. "*You* have to too. And you have to keep trying. That's more important than anything."

We sat there for a few minutes while I sniffled and pretended I wasn't wiping frustrated tears on the sleeve of my T-shirt. I peeked over at my dad. He was sitting with his arms wrapped around his knees, staring at the playground across the parking lot, a little smile on his face. "The funny thing about the ollie is, once you do it, you won't be able to believe you couldn't get it before. It's just…something's gotta click. But don't worry. It will." He pushed himself up from the ground and stood, holding out a hand to me. "I think we've done enough for now. Let's pick it up again tomorrow." I grabbed his hand without thinking. It was so easy to let his strength pull me up. I dropped his hand abruptly and stared at the ground.

"I mean, if you want to keep at it. Do you?"

I could hear the uncertainty in his voice, and I jerked my eyes up. "Yes," I said. "I want to."

He nodded. "Good." He dropped his board and put one foot on it and then turned back to me. "Really, Daf. You might learn tomorrow or it might take a few weeks, but you're going to land an ollie for sure. Once you do that, we'll shoot for a kickflip." He pointed at me. "*And* you're going to drop in at a Silver Sesh before you leave."

"Really?" I said.

He looked me right in the eye. "Really."

On the way back we pushed and glided faster than we had on our way to the park. The air smelled of barbecue and jasmine, and I matched my dad's strides, staying right behind him. I had no reason to believe him. How did he know what I could or couldn't accomplish? He didn't know that I'd be gone soon...maybe I wouldn't have time to learn all that stuff. But he'd seemed so sure when he said I would. For some reason hearing him say it made me think: *Maybe. Maybe I really could.*

13

I flipped my pillow over and tried to feel sleepy. My brain was going in circles. I kept telling myself: *Don't count on him. It was just one skating lesson.*

But I also kept thinking of my dad's serious expression as he showed me how to fall and how there wasn't a trace of impatience in his face when I messed up the ollie, over and over. I thought of the way he had said "Another sesh tomorrow?" as I headed to bed. I'd nodded, and he turned away from me quickly, but not before I caught the big smile on his face.

I wasn't sure how I felt about any of it. It was a

relief to hear my phone buzz and see a text from Mom pop up.

> Hey sweets! I have a few minutes, thought I'd text my girl. How's it going with your dad?

My finger hesitated. She'd never loved the idea of me being a skater. I wasn't sure if I wanted to tell her about our lessons. Besides, it was only one. It's OK, I typed. How's life as a movie star?

She sent me a photo: her at a restaurant with five other people standing at the end of the table, their arms around each other.

> This is right after the chef insisted we all have rabbit for dinner. Couldn't help but think of old Bugs 😷 🐰 🙊

I laughed. Bugs was my pet bunny when I was in first grade. Mom always pretended to hate him, but she'd cried right along with me when he died.

> I can't believe you ate one of Bugs's relatives! 🩶 🍪

I zoomed in on the picture. Mom had warned me she might have to change her hair color, and she had: It was now a buttery blond. Everyone in the shot was smiling. I recognized three of them—not because I'd ever met them but because I'd seen them in movies. It hit me again: She was working with famous actors like she'd always dreamed of. It caused a strange dip in my stomach. I should be glad for her. I *was*. It was just... seeing her like that, with these people I didn't know— famous people—made her seem so far away. Like now she was different somehow.

> Your hair looks great! Looks like you have a lot of cool new friends.

None of them compare to you, Babygirl. I miss you so much! I can't believe we have to be away from each other for so long.

I smiled at my phone.

> I know! I'm really excited about coming to Prague. 😉 Oh, and seeing you too! 😂

My smile faded as the three dots that meant she was typing appeared and then disappeared, then appeared again. Finally, her message popped up.

> I still haven't asked! 😫
> I promise I will soon!

I stared at the message. She hadn't even asked? Didn't she know how much I was counting on escaping? I started to text her that very thought, but when I read it over, "escape" didn't seem like the right word anymore. While I was still thinking about how to put it, another message popped up.

> Don't be mad! I PROMISE to
> talk to the producer as soon
> as humanly possible. Gtg
> now tho 🖤 🖤 🖤

I sent her a good-night kiss emoji, relieved not to have to talk about my dad. It was enough that Mom was figuring out a way for me to go see her.

My dad and I headed back to the school the next afternoon.

"Should I work on my ollie some more?" I asked.

"Let's forget about the ollie for today." My dad took off his cap and scratched his head. "Maybe let's do some freestyle stuff, just have some fun." He bent down and laid his board wheels up, over the tips of his toes. Then he jumped, flipped the board over, and landed on top of it. He tic-tacked back and forth. "Give it a try."

I set my board up and then jumped and landed on it, just like my dad had.

"First try!" my dad said. "Amazing."

"Is it really a trick though?" I asked. I did it again and couldn't hold back a smile. It was pretty fun, whatever it was.

"Sure," he said. "I mean, it's freestyle. It's not going to get you in the Olympics, but it definitely counts as a trick. You know, Rodney Mullen is probably the most famous freestyler of all time, and he invented the ollie."

"No, that's wrong," I said. "Alan 'Ollie' Gelfand did."

Dad flashed his dimple at me. "How do you know that?"

I'd learned that fact specifically to impress him when I was nine, but of course I wasn't going to admit that. I shrugged. "I just know."

"Well, you're not wrong, but Rodney Mullen's really

the one who made it popular. Anyway, how about this?" He demonstrated Arlo's trick, the wraparound. Then he showed me where to put my feet and how to flip the board around. I didn't get it on the first try, but it didn't take me too long.

"Okay, now I think you're ready for a shuvit," my dad said.

"But you have to ollie to do that." I knew what a pop shuvit was, of course: You spun your board 180 degrees as you jumped in the air and then landed on it.

"For a pop shuvit, yes, but you can do it on the ground without the pop."

He demonstrated turning his board around 180 degrees and broke it down for me step by step. I obediently practiced doing the rotation without landing on the board. It took me a while, but I got it. Then he showed me again, and this time he broke down the part where I'd land with my two feet on the board.

I got it on the first try.

"Daf! That's amazing!" My dad moved closer to me like he was going to give me a hug. Without thinking, I jerked away. "That was pretty cool," I said quickly, hoping he hadn't noticed.

"It was," my dad agreed. Maybe he hadn't. "Now do it again."

But I couldn't get it the next few times. "I think it was just a fluke," I muttered, but my dad told me to keep trying. When I finally landed it again, his grin was as big as mine. "See? I knew you had it in you," he said.

We skated around the playground and the parking lot, and I did a shuvit over and over, stopping every once in a while to make sure I really had the wrap-around down too. I grinned as my dad ollied over the speed bumps and kickflipped up and onto the concrete wall, but for once I wasn't longing to do those tricks myself. I was happy with my shuvit. It was a legit trick! I couldn't wait to show Arlo.

When my dad called out from across the playground that we should start home for dinner, I skated over, ready to head toward the hole in the fence. "Wait a second, Daf." He let out a funny little laugh. "I have to tell you something."

"Oh. Okay." He sounded nervous, and that made me nervous. Was he going to back out of teaching me to skate now that I'd learned a trick? Or worse: Was he going to try to make me talk to him about my feelings?

He sighed. "I don't know why this is so hard," he muttered, shaking his head. "Can we sit?"

We walked over to the concrete wall. I sat down and braced myself for whatever was coming.

"Okay," my dad said. "You know I'm an alcoholic, right?"

"Yeah, but...you're better now, right?" I hated the way my voice shook. He was going to tell me I couldn't count on him, I knew it.

"I am, kind of. With alcoholics, it's an always thing. I'll never not be an alcoholic, but I'm in recovery. I haven't had a drink in over two years."

I nodded warily. "That's good."

"It's a start. But what I wanted to talk to you about is there's this thing we have to do, called making amends. It's where you make up for all the messed-up stuff you did to all the people you let down." He paused. "You're one of those people. You're the most important one, in fact. So I'd like to make amends to you. For all the times I wasn't there."

I grabbed my left elbow and stared at the ground. No way could I meet his eyes. "It's okay." It wasn't. Of course it wasn't. But I sure didn't want to talk about it.

"No, it's not." I could feel him turning toward me,

but I still couldn't manage to lift my gaze. "Look, Daf, to me, making amends is more than saying I'm sorry. Sorry doesn't cut it. Amends means taking action, doing something to make it up to you." He laughed. "I have this one friend in the program, he does it by making pies for people. *So* many pies." I didn't crack a smile, and he cleared his throat. "So even though I can't really make up for those years of your life when I wasn't around, I'd like to make amends by teaching you how to skate. However much time it takes, whatever you want to do, till you learn everything you want to learn. But only if you want to, of course." He paused. "Do you think you do?"

It wasn't at all what I'd expected him to say. I chewed my lower lip. It had been one thing to ask him to give me lessons, but saying yes to what he was offering...that would mean trusting him. Could I do that? I closed my eyes briefly. Maybe I could trust him for now. I forced myself to look at his face. "But I'm never going to learn everything I want to learn," I said.

He flashed his dimple at me. "And *that's* how I know you're a real skater. All right. How about we work on stuff till the end of summer, and then we keep going whenever I see you again. Which, if I have anything to say about it, will be often and soon. Okay?"

I studied the toes of my Vans and felt guilty that he thought I'd be here all summer. I reminded myself that he'd promised this before. I rubbed my elbow again and pictured the blood dripping down my knee. I tried to conjure up that cold, strong determination not to let him in, not to count on him for anything.

None of it worked.

"Okay." I swallowed and nodded. "It's a deal."

14

The next day, Grandma Kate took me to Alcatraz Island. At the end of the tour they locked us up in a prison cell to see how it felt. It was awful, but she and I got the giggles, then got them even worse when people stared at us. We finished our excursion with ice cream again, but we were having such a good time, Grandma suggested we have dinner at her house and called my dad to invite him too.

Grandpa barbecued some ribs and put me in charge of peeling the potatoes so Grandma could mash them. My dad arrived when dinner was ready, carrying a pie from a bakery. He'd left for an interview early that morning, so I hadn't seen him since our skate lesson the day before. I tried to pretend things hadn't changed between us. I didn't even say hello to him, just watched him put the pie on the counter and kiss Grandma on the cheek.

But when we sat down at dinner, I blurted out, "My dad's teaching me how to do some skate tricks."

"Well, isn't that nice now?" Grandpa said, raising his eyebrows in the direction of my dad.

"You wear a helmet, don't you?" Grandma asked. "Remember that friend of yours who fell on his head? What was his name? Marcus? He was never the same after that."

My dad waved her comment away. "It was a concussion, Mom. He was fine, eventually."

She frowned. "Still. You do wear a helmet, don't you, Daphne?" She widened her eyes at my dad.

"She wears a helmet," my dad said.

"Because Eden would have a fit if she found out she wasn't being safe—"

"Mom. She wears one."

Grandma nodded, and then we talked about Alcatraz and my dad's job hunt and listened to Grandma and Grandpa debate about whether they should get chickens to keep in their backyard. After dinner, we all sat around in their living room and ate pie while Lady sprawled on the rug in the middle of the room.

Then Grandma Kate leaned forward and grabbed a big brown book off the coffee table. "Daphne, you were asking about your dad as a little boy, so I pulled this photo album out." She opened it over both our laps.

"You were asking about me, huh?" my dad asked. The couch sank on the other side of me as he sat down. I pretended not to hear him.

"Who's that?" I asked Grandma, pointing to a young man I was pretty sure was my grandpa. We went through it slowly, Grandma narrating each page—Christmas photos, birthday parties, vacation pictures. And then the family portraits gave way to pictures of my dad skating. At first they were snapshots, and then the photos took up the whole page, with different versions of my dad and a bunch of guys on some big ramp, skate logos everywhere—on their shirts, hats, boards. "That's when I started getting some flow," my dad said, leaning over to tap on one of the pictures. "I thought I was going to get a sponsorship any day. I thought I was on the road to being a professional skater."

"What happened?" I asked.

My dad's eyes fell to his lap, and Grandma said, "Never mind that." She tried to flip the page, but my dad stopped her.

"It's okay, Mom. What happened was, I blew it," he told me. "I was supposed to be a good representative of the brand, and I didn't keep my part of the bargain."

Like you didn't keep your bargain with me, I thought. I leaned over the picture, trying to see if there was something in my dad's face that explained why he let everyone down so easily back then. I glanced up at him, hoping to see a difference. He looked older, that was for sure. Was that enough?

"It's just a shame we had to miss out on seeing Daphne all these years because of a few mistakes." Grandma sighed.

"Mom," my dad said. "Stop." He stood up and took the photo album from our laps and put it back on the shelf. "It's getting late anyway. We should head home. I want to send out some more résumés tonight."

"Still no bites, huh?" Grandpa said from his chair.

My dad shook his head. "Nope."

"I'm sure something will turn up, any day now," Grandma said, walking us to the door.

"I hope you're right." His shoulders sagged. I thought

of the way he encouraged me during our skate lessons: calmly, like there was no question I'd eventually be able to do what I wanted to do. I kind of wished I could do that for him right now, but I didn't know what to say.

My dad and I walked to the car in silence.

15

I was in bed, paging through an old *Thrasher* magazine I'd found on my dad's bookshelf, admiring the photos of all the cool tricks and noticing there were zero girls in any of them.

Bang! Something crashed, and a loud shout came from the kitchen.

It's weird the way time slows down when you're afraid. As I jumped out of bed and ran toward the kitchen, all these thoughts ran through my mind: Had my dad hurt himself? What if something fell on top of him? Would I be able to get him out? Should I call an ambulance?

But when I got there, he was fine. At least, physically. He was standing in the middle of the kitchen, staring down at his laptop on the floor. When he saw me, he bent over quickly to pick it up and clutched it to his chest. "It's okay," he said. "It's not broken."

I stared at him. His eyes were wide with shock—or maybe even fear. It was like he couldn't believe that someone had dropped his computer on the floor and that he'd been the someone who'd done it.

"Are *you* okay?" I asked. But instead of going to him as you would if you were worried about someone, I stepped back. He was acting so strange.

My dad nodded like he hadn't really heard me. He placed the laptop on the table. "Yeah. I'm okay." He shot me a smile that didn't reach his eyes. "Just another job thing." His jaw was clenched so tight I could see the twitch in his cheek. "It's fine."

"Okay." But I stood there. It clearly wasn't fine, but I didn't know what to do about it. This wasn't like when Mom didn't get a part. A hug and a bowl of ice cream wasn't going to make my dad feel better right now.

"Hey." He drummed his fingers on the back of the chair. "You want to go to the school? Skate a little?"

"Right now?"

"Yes, right now. I could use a break."

"But it's dark. And I'm in my pajamas."

"The school has lights, and you can change. Or don't, I don't care." He stopped drumming and gripped the back of the chair so hard his knuckles turned white. He seemed like he was about to explode. "Let's just go."

"Um. Are you sure you're all right?"

"*Yes*. I'm fine," he said through clenched teeth. He didn't sound fine. Not at all. And I was scared.

That's when I realized what must be happening. Tears sprang to my eyes, and I blinked them away. "Just a minute," I said. My voice sounded weak and shaky, but I didn't care. I hurried to my room and found my phone, grateful now that Mom had programmed my grandma's number in there. "Grandma?" I said when she picked up.

"Daphne. Are you safe?"

"Yes," I said. How did she know to ask me that? "It's just that my dad—"

"Is he well enough to talk?"

"Well enough?" I didn't understand, but she sounded frantic.

"Put him on the phone, Daphne. Let me speak to your father."

I took the phone out to the kitchen, holding it in front of me like it was some kind of shield that would guard me from this scary version of my dad. "Grandma wants to talk to you," I said. I laid the phone on the table and moved back to the doorway and watched him.

My dad seemed to shrink then. He sank onto the chair and closed his eyes for a second. When he opened them again, he looked so, so tired. He reached for my phone and leaned his head in one hand. "Hi." His voice was low, the edge I'd heard before gone. "We're fine.... No, it's a job thing.... I know. You're right. I'm sorry.... I'll call him.... Nah, Mom, you don't have to. I know you're already in bed. I'll get Gus.... Okay. I'm sorry.... I won't. I'm sorry." He hung up and lifted his head to look at me. "Sorry, Daf," he said softly. "I didn't mean to scare you."

I stayed in the doorway. I had to ask him. "Are you drunk?"

"What? No!" He laughed. "You've been with me all night, you know I haven't been drinking." The smile fell from his face abruptly. "But you're on the right track. I'm struggling. I'd give anything to have a drink right now."

I hugged myself and tried to swallow the lump in my throat. "Are you going to?"

He shook his head. "Nope. I'm going to call my sponsor, and I'm going to go to a meeting, and I'm going to have Gus come and get you. Is that all right? I didn't want to get my parents out of bed. You okay with staying over there tonight?" He ran his hand over his face.

"Okay." My fear was fading, but I was confused. "I thought you didn't have a sponsor anymore? And why are you going to a meeting? Is it another job interview?"

He looked puzzled for a second, then laughed softly. "Not a skating sponsor. No, it's my AA sponsor. I'll explain in a minute. Let me make some phone calls."

I nodded. He took his phone and went into the living room. I sat down at the table and waited, squeezing my phone so tight that my hand started to sweat.

After a while he came back. His face seemed less tight, but his eyes were sad. "It's all set." He sat down at the table with me. "I'm sorry, Daf. I know that was scary what just happened there. I kind of lost it. I was trying not to, but I did."

I nodded, but I didn't really get it.

"So, you know what AA is, right?"

I nodded again. "Kind of. It helps you not drink?"

"Right. That's what the meeting is. It's a bunch of alcoholics who get together and share their stories, support each other as they're trying to stay sober. And my sponsor is someone who's been through it already, been doing it longer than I have anyway. He's the person I call when I'm in trouble. To help get through it. You'll meet him."

Not long after that, Gus came over, and then John, my dad's sponsor. He didn't look like the type of person who'd be friends with my dad. He was an older Asian man wearing a crisp white button-down shirt and black pants, like a businessman. He waved to Gus and introduced himself to me. He promised to take good care of my dad.

"Rusty made you a bed on the couch," Gus said quietly as he opened the door to his house. "Arlo's already asleep."

"I'm sorry if we woke you—"

"Stop right there," Gus said, holding his hand up. "I told your dad a long time ago that if you got to stay with him for the summer, I'd have his back—and yours. I meant it. You're welcome here anytime."

"Oh. Okay. Thanks." It was strange to be here at night, and without Arlo. I wished I could go back to my dad's and curl up in my own bed.

"Tell you what, let's have some hot chocolate." Gus led me into his kitchen, which, unlike my dad's, had already been remodeled into an airy space with a huge window overlooking the backyard. He had little twinkling lights strung up out there that illuminated the yard just enough to see the silhouette of the bowl. I stared out at it.

Gus poured some milk into a pot and measured chocolate powder into it. "I'm not much for sweets, but there's something about hot chocolate. It's the perfect thing to have when unexpected things happen at nighttime."

I kept looking out the window. I wondered how Gus was still friends with my dad after all this time. Didn't it bother him that he had this...problem?

"You all right there, Daphne?" Gus asked after a while.

"Have you ever seen my dad drunk?" I swung around so I could see his face. Gus calmly stirred the chocolate, the metal spoon scraping against the bottom of the pot. He didn't act shocked by my question. I was kind of hoping he would. But he did take a few seconds to answer.

"Yes," Gus said. "I have."

"If it's so bad for him, why didn't you stop him?"

"Well, when we were young, we all used to drink quite a bit," Gus said. "I didn't really understand Joe had a problem at first. By the time I did, it was too late."

"What do you mean, too late? If you'd told him he needed to stop earlier, do you think he would have?" I couldn't ask my mom these questions, or Grandma either. But Gus seemed like he didn't mind talking about it.

He smiled and shook his head. "It doesn't really work like that. Other people telling him to stop—and I did, by the way, many times—it doesn't have an effect. Addiction is complicated. And there's not really anything anyone can do until the person who's addicted is ready to stop. Got any more questions?"

I did. I had so many questions. I picked the one that was bothering me the most. "Yes. How come, if you all drank, my dad was the only one who had a problem with it?"

Gus shook his head again. "No one really knows the answer to that. Could be brain chemistry or genetics or just bad luck."

"Do you think he's going to drink tonight?"

"Nope." Gus joined me at the window and handed me a mug of creamy hot chocolate. "Careful, it's hot. I can tell you your dad won't drink tonight because he's with John. They'll go to a late-night meeting, and if that's not enough, John will stay with him until your dad's okay."

We both stared out at the silhouette of the bowl, sipping our chocolate. After a while, Gus said, "My dad was an alcoholic too."

I turned to him. "Really?"

Gus nodded. "He didn't stop drinking until he was much older than your dad. It took him a few tries." He took a sip of chocolate. "I get how hard it is to forgive your dad for not being there."

I shrugged. Did my dad talk to Gus about me? Did he tell him how mean I was to him? "Did you ever forgive your dad?"

Gus nodded. "Eventually. But it took me a long time." He hesitated. "How you doing with it?"

I shot Gus a look. I knew he'd report to my dad whatever I told him. "Better, I guess."

He laughed. "Well, that's nice and vague. Okay, let me put you on the spot about something else: How am I doing with Arlo?"

I smiled. I didn't expect that. "Good, I think."

Gus laughed. "I guess I can't really ask you much more than that, huh? I don't want to break any kind of friend code. I'm glad you two are getting along though."

"Yeah," I said. "Arlo's cool." I was suddenly exhausted. "Um, would you mind if I went to bed?"

"Not at all."

I slipped into the bed on the couch. As tired as I was, I thought I'd lie awake and wonder and worry about my dad. But I fell right asleep.

16

When I opened my eyes, I could hear my dad's voice in the kitchen. I sat up on the couch.

"Maybe Edy was right," my dad was saying. I leaned forward, straining to hear.

"Nah, man." That was Gus. "You got this. Nothing happened. It's okay."

"But, Gus, she called my mom. She shouldn't have had to do that. And what if she hadn't?" My dad's voice quavered.

"Things don't always happen like they should." That was Rusty. "We all know that. Mistakes happen. You just have to move on. You're doing fine."

I stood up and was about to tiptoe closer so I could eavesdrop better when my dad peeked around the kitchen doorway. "Hey," he said. "How'd you sleep?"

"Fine." I stretched my arms up, pretending like I just woke up.

"You hungry? Gus is making pancakes."

Rusty came out then and smiled at me. "Good morning, Daphne! I was just about to get Arlo up."

We all crowded into the kitchen, and Gus served us stacks of pancakes. Rusty must have told Arlo what had happened the night before, because he kept shooting me worried looks. In fact, everyone was watching me, especially my dad. It was driving me nuts! I finished my pancakes and put down my fork. "Can we go down to the school and skate?" I said. "All of us?"

"Yes!" Rusty clapped her hands. "Great idea! Let's do it." We all grabbed our boards, even Rusty. "I only push along"—she smiled at me—"so don't expect any tricks like you all do!" I liked the way she wasn't self-conscious about it.

It was fun skating with everyone. The clatter of five boards on the sidewalk made anyone who was outside turn and look. I felt part of something.

At the school, my dad made me show Arlo, Rusty, and Gus my wraparound and then my shuvit, and they all cheered. Then Arlo and Gus tried to get Rusty to go over a speed bump. When she said she was too scared, they each held one of her hands to help her over. It was a good thing too, because she stumbled off her board, and they had to hold her up. She laughed and said she wanted to try again. My dad and I stood off to the side, watching them. "Hey," he said. "You want to work on your ollie for a while?"

"Sure," I said. We skated over to our favorite asphalt crack.

My dad hopped off his board. "And last night too. We should talk about that."

I bent over and placed my board in the crack. "We don't have to," I mumbled, not looking up.

"We kinda do, Daf." He paused, but I stayed crouched, resting my hands on the deck of my board. "I know it was scary and uncomfortable, but I have to say this to you: I'm sorry. I'm trying really hard to stay on track, but this job search thing really gets me down sometimes. It feels like I'm not getting anywhere no matter how hard I try." He let out a long sigh. "That's no excuse for me losing control last night, but it happened, and I'm sorry."

I rose to my feet slowly and glanced quickly up at my dad's face and back down again. "It's okay."

"And one more thing, Daf. You know it's not your fault, right? What happened last night? That was all me."

He stood there like he was waiting for me to say something else, but I didn't know what to say. "Can we work on my ollie now?" I asked. I stood on my board and bounced my knees a little.

For a second I thought he was going to insist we keep talking about serious stuff, but then he said, "Sure." He leaned down and grabbed my left foot. "You want to move this back a little toward the tail, just behind the front truck bolts." He stood up. "Now, I know it's corny, talking about determination and stuff. But it's the great thing about skating: It reminds you how to live your life. You have to fall a million times, but that's part of it."

"Let me guess." I rolled my eyes at him. "It's all about getting back up again?"

"Told you it was corny." He laughed. "But yeah, that's it."

I bounced on my board again, thinking about how I'd wanted to encourage my dad last night. "Can I tell you something?"

"Sure," he said, but his forehead creased in worry.

"I just want you to remember." I made my voice serious and deep. "With patience and determination and not being afraid to fall, you're going to find a job." I poked him in the chest. "But *you* have to believe it too."

My dad threw back his head and laughed. "Tossing my own words back at me, very funny." His smile faded, and his eyes softened. "Thanks, Daf. That actually helps." I thought he was going to get all mushy on me, but he pointed to my board. "Keep trying."

I nodded, glad to get back to skating, but something inside me that had been tight ever since I'd heard the bang of his laptop on the floor last night relaxed a bit. The truth was, I liked what was happening between me and my dad, corny encouragement and all.

So I tried to ollie.

I tried and I tried and I tried. I'd try to lift my back foot in the air after the pop, but I was always too slow. Or I'd try to slide my front foot and end up falling backward. Or I just got tangled up in my feet.

I forgot my dad was there and totally focused on

my board. I got so I could pop it up pretty well. I did it enough times that I figured I could slide my other foot at the same time.

"Pop, slide, jump," I kept whispering to myself. I tried again. And again and again.

Then it happened: All four wheels lifted about an inch off the ground at the same time.

"That's it!" my dad whooped.

"That counts?"

"Yes!" he said.

"But it was so small," I protested.

"Hey. Your board was airborne, and you landed on it. That's an ollie! The more you do it, the higher you'll get, but you did the hardest part: You got the first one! Now keep going."

I didn't do it the next time, but I did it the time after that and then again, a little higher. I stopped and looked at my dad.

"What?" he said.

I didn't want to tell him I hadn't trusted him. I didn't even know for sure that I hadn't, not until just now. But he'd taught me how to ollie, exactly as he'd promised. "Nothing," I said.

Maybe he guessed a little of what I was thinking, because he said, "I told you you'd get it. I never doubted it."

"I caught it on camera!" Arlo was walking toward us, looking down at the screen in his hands. "You want to see?"

"You were filming me?" I put my hands on my hips. But I couldn't be too mad. I'd landed an ollie!

"It's actually a good way to learn how to perfect your form," my dad said. "Watch yourself. Critique. See what you can change."

"You want to check it out?" Arlo asked, extending his camera.

I cringed. "I hate watching myself on video."

"You weren't always that way." My dad smiled. "I remember taking a video of you one Christmas. You could barely talk. I filmed you singing this little song, and you wanted to watch yourself over and over. It was pretty cute."

I stared at him, trying to imagine him and Mom getting along well enough that he'd come over on Christmas. I didn't remember it. It was strange to think he did.

"All right, let's keep going," my dad said. "Doing an ollie on a crack standing still is one thing, but I know you want to get where you can move with it."

Rusty and Gus and Arlo headed back home, but my dad and I kept at it.

The sun was high in the sky when he said, "I think we better call it. I should get some emails out."

When we got home, I was pretty sweaty and went to take a shower. Afterward, I came back to the kitchen to find something to eat. My dad was on his computer at the kitchen table again. He turned when I came in. "I got a second interview for a job!"

"Really?"

"Yes. And I want to thank you, Daf. I've been feeling pretty discouraged about it, but it actually helped a lot when you reminded me that I just have to keep at it."

I shrugged, a little embarrassed. "I'm really happy for you, Dad."

He raised an eyebrow at me, his dimple poking through his cheek.

"What?"

He grinned and shook his head. "Nothing."

But I knew he'd noticed.

I'd just called him Dad.

17

The next day, I woke up worried. What if my ollie was a fluke? I didn't even change out of my pajamas, just slipped my Vans on, grabbed my board, and opened the glass door to the tiny backyard.

It wasn't a fluke. I could still ollie! I did it over and over and over, trying to get more air under my board.

I didn't realize how loud I was until Dad poked his head out the door.

"Hey, Daf," he said, running a hand through his rumpled hair. "You might want to wait till it's a little later before you start that."

"Oh." I stopped, one foot on my board and the other on the ground. "Sorry."

His face cracked into a smile. "You're really getting it down! It's a little early is all." He gestured to the fence that bordered his house and Gus's. "We get enough complaints about Gus's bowl without making a bunch of noise at seven in the morning. Maybe head out to the school? Or if you can wait till later, I'll go with you. I have a few things I gotta do this morning."

"Can we have another lesson later?"

"Sure."

"Okay. I think I'll go to the school for now." I got dressed. But instead of going all the way to the school, I stopped at the skate park.

I hopped off my board and stood at the entrance. Even though it was so early, five guys, probably high school age, were skating around. I watched them for a while. At the top of three steps was a Jersey barrier, one of those things they use to divide roads. One guy kept trying to sail over it—stairs and barrier both. He'd get over it but would fall off his board when he landed, every time, hard. He'd lie on the concrete for a few seconds and then get back up and go for it again. A couple of his friends stood on the edge encouraging him, and another guy was skating the mini ramp. It wasn't like any of them were especially great skaters.

But they still intimidated me.

I turned and headed back home, disappointed in myself.

When I got to my dad's house, I stopped on the sidewalk. My stomach felt wound tight, like a skater was in there bending her knees and getting ready to ollie but she was frozen, unable to lift off. I needed to get some air under her.

I looked at the house. Dad was going to skate with me later today, but I wanted to do this now. I pulled out my phone and texted Arlo. **You awake?**

After a minute I could see the dots that meant he was typing, but before his response came through I sent another text: **Will you go to the skate park with me? Now? I'm outside.**

A few minutes later Arlo emerged from the front door. He was dressed, but I could tell by his tousled hair that he had just woken up. He opened his mouth like he was going to say something then saw the look on my face and nodded. "One sec."

He went and got his board and camera. We took off.

I thought a friend by my side would give me the

little extra courage I needed. But when we got back to the park, my shoulders sagged. The same five guys were there. In the skate bowl in my stomach, the skater unwound herself and gave up. My feet froze. I couldn't move them to enter the park.

Arlo followed my gaze over to the older boys at the half-pipe. "Let's go to the outer area. There aren't any people over there."

"No," I growled.

Arlo lifted his hands in surrender. "Fine. You were the one who brought us here."

He was right. I knew I wasn't making sense. I *wanted* to go into the park.

I just couldn't.

Thinking about it made my face heat up with shame. I rubbed my elbow and stared at the ground, grinding my teeth together. I felt so idiotic. I couldn't meet Arlo's eyes. "Sorry," I said.

"Okaayy." Arlo sighed. "Let's go over there." He pointed to our old picnic table. We leaned against the table, facing the skate park. Arlo took his camera out of its case and pointed it in various directions, looking through the viewfinder. I laid my skateboard over my lap, my eyes lifting every once in a while over to the skaters. Despite everything, the scrape of wheels on concrete pulled at me, an invitation I wished I didn't have to say no to.

"You obviously want to skate in the skate park," Arlo said. "So why won't you?"

I spun one of the wheels on my board, then stopped it, then spun it again. "I just don't think I can"—I lifted my chin in the direction of the skate park—"skate with them."

Arlo laughed. "Of course you can. You've been skating with me practically every day since we met. What's the difference?"

How could I explain it to him? I counted off on my fingers, pointing them at Arlo. "I don't do any tricks. I can't drop in. I can barely ollie." One, two, three excellent reasons.

"It's not like someone's grading you," Arlo said. "No one's even paying attention. Everyone does their own thing."

"Yeah, right," I said, so much sarcasm dripping out of my voice that Arlo flinched.

"Whatever," he said. "I was just trying to help." He bent over his camera so his hair hung over his face.

Great. Now I'd hurt his feelings. "Sorry," I said quickly. "It's just...skaters *say* that. My dad told me the exact same thing when I was little, that it's all about having fun and getting up after you fall and doing your own thing—but it's not true." I shook my head.

Arlo lifted his head and brushed his hair back. "How do you know that if you never go to the parks?"

I stuck my feet out and studied my Vans. The edges were getting all scuffed up like Dad said they would. "I've been to skate parks. But the last time I went to one it didn't work out so well," I said in a low voice.

"Why? What happened?"

I'd never told anyone all the details of that day, not even when I told Sam how I broke my arm. But Arlo was looking at me, just curious. He'd already seen the panic that came over me at the thought of skating in the skate park. I was pretty sure if anyone would understand, it'd be him.

So I told him everything: how I'd loved to watch my dad skate and how happy I was when he gave me my board on my ninth birthday. I even told him about the chant: *Ollie, nollie, kickflip, shuvit. Backside, frontside, fakie, grind.*

Then I told him about the Skate Park Disaster.

When I finished, Arlo let out a long sigh. "I know," I said quickly, before he could say it. "It was stupid to go there by myself. And I shouldn't have been so stupid to try dropping in without knowing how. I deserved to break my arm. It was stup—"

"Will you stop saying it was stupid?" Arlo broke in.

I spun the wheels on my board and didn't look at him.

"You didn't do anything wrong! Those guys were jerks! Most people aren't like that." He let out a sharp laugh. "No, wait. I take it back—you did do something wrong. You let them get to you."

I clamped my hands over the wheels and felt the slight burn as they stopped spinning. I didn't say anything, but I was listening.

"I hate to break it to you, but you've been wasting your time. You didn't need to avoid skate parks just because of that one time."

I stared at him. It sounded so simple, but hearing him say it out loud made me realize he was right: Those boys were mean to me! They ran away after I got hurt! Of course they were jerks! It was so obvious, I should have understood it a long time ago. But somehow I needed to hear Arlo say it first. I almost smiled at how easy the realization came.

But I didn't smile.

Because, despite the truth of what he said, the awfulness of that day still weighed on me. I studied the bottom of my board again, tracing my fingers around the outline of the flame sticker. "I guess...I mean, you're right. But it's really more that...you know, my dad didn't come." I swallowed. I did not want to cry. "He said he'd be there, and he never showed up. He never apologized or explained when I talked to him on the phone. I kept waiting for him to but..." I shook my head. "I never even saw him again until I came to Oakland this summer."

"Whoa." Arlo whistled. "That really sucks."

"Yeah." This time I did manage a smile. "It sucks big-time."

And then, for some reason, we both laughed. It didn't seem like I should feel any better just because we both agreed my dad blew it. But I did.

When our laughter died down, Arlo fiddled with a setting on his camera. "Can I tell you something? Since we're talking about parents sucking?" He didn't look up when he spoke.

"Sure."

"My mom lied."

I stared at him blankly. "Lied? About what?"

"The landlord didn't make us move. He's kind of a jerk, and he definitely wasn't wild about having a kid in his building, but he never told my mom we had to move out. She told Gus that so he'd ask us to move in with him."

"Oh." I sucked in a breath. "Wow."

"Yeah," he said. "Messed up, right?"

I didn't know what to say. If I agreed with him, I was saying his mom was messed up, and that wasn't a good answer. On the other hand, it *was* kind of messed up. "That's why you were mad at her the other day?"

Arlo nodded. "I told her she should tell Gus the truth, and when she said she wouldn't, well... I hate it when she tries to push her way in on people. I kind of went off on her." Arlo sighed. "She started crying."

"What are you going to do?"

"Nothing. She's afraid he'll break up with her if he finds out she lied."

"Do you think he would? He obviously likes you guys a lot."

Arlo shrugged. "I don't know. Maybe? Just my luck, she finally met a guy who thinks it's important to be honest." He tried to make it sound like a joke, but I could tell he was really worried. "Anyway, I didn't want to keep hassling her, because what if Gus does break up with her? We'd have to move out."

"*That's* why you weren't excited about moving in,"

I said. Arlo nodded. He was still scrolling through the pictures on his camera, but I could tell he wasn't really seeing them. He had just made me feel so much better. I needed to do the same for him. "Gus is so nice though," I said. "And I think he's really happy to have you there."

"He does seem cool with it, right?" Arlo said.

"He really does."

Arlo finally cracked a smile. "I just hate it when my mom cries."

"Crying moms are the worst," I agreed. Then I pointed at him. "You could always rub her feet!"

"That," Arlo said, "is one thing I will never do." He stopped fussing with his camera. "Hey, you want to see something?" He put the camera in front of my face and pressed a button. The screen was small and the sun was shining on it, so I had to lean in close and shade my eyes. It was a pair of feet and a skateboard. *My* board, I realized. I watched as the feet—my feet—tried to ollie but messed up a little differently each time until, much faster than I remember it happening in real life, the board lifted! Then it lifted again, this time in slow motion.

I couldn't stop a smile from creeping across my face. "That's cool," I admitted, handing him back the camera. "The way it built up. You made it tell a story."

"Exactly!" Arlo exclaimed. "I have to get you doing a full ollie to finish it off. I was thinking—" He stopped abruptly.

I laughed. "I can tell you're dying to ask me to be in your movie again."

"I didn't say anything!" But he was smiling.

I shrugged. "You can do it if you want."

"Really?" Arlo sprang to his feet.

"I guess."

"I have to be honest: It's not all going to be footwork. That would be boring. Your face will be in there too."

"It's okay. I think I can handle it."

"Of course you can! It's in your blood! You were born to be a star, just like your mom."

"Ha ha," I said, pushing myself to my feet. "Are you ready to go?"

"Sure. And Daphne," Arlo said, "don't worry about the skate park thing. I'm sure you'll get there in time."

"I know," I said, flashing him a smile. "We're going right now."

Arlo's eyes got so big I had to laugh. Then I threw down my board and hopped onto it. I didn't look back to see if Arlo was with me.

I knew he was.

18

I didn't even slow down at the gate. I skated right on in.

I headed to some easy transitions and pumped over them. It wasn't so different from the speed bumps in the school parking lot. Arlo and I skated the mini ramps and then moved to the small bowl. It wasn't fancy, we weren't doing tricks, but I was here, skating in the skate park. The tightness in my stomach had finally loosened. My inner skater had been freed!

I laughed out loud at my own silliness and skated over to some flat ground so I could work on my ollie. I ignored Arlo when he came over and started filming me. I did it over and over—it never got boring, because every time was different. Sometimes I landed it, sometimes I fell off my board, sometimes I got a little higher. I stopped once to look around. No one but Arlo was paying attention to me. The high school guys were still trying to get over that Jersey barrier.

I lost track of time until Arlo emerged from behind his camera to ask, "Is it boba time yet?"

I could have stayed longer, but when I pulled my phone out to check the time, I realized we'd been skating for hours. "Sure," I said.

I couldn't hold back my huge smile as we skated over to the Quickly. It wasn't anything special as far as skating went. I hadn't done any sick tricks. But I'd skated at the skate park, and nothing bad had happened. I couldn't wait to ask Dad if we could move our practice sessions there.

It finally felt like a place I belonged.

Over the next few days, Arlo and I went to the skate park every day, and Dad joined us there after he was done with whatever he had to do that day. I was working on moving as I ollied instead of just doing it in one spot. Dad taught me how to rock to fakie too, and I loved skating up onto the coping of the quarter-pipe, rocking forward, and then sliding back down again with the back end of my board leading. I'd throw in my shuvit every once in a while to mix it up. Gus and Rusty came by sometimes, and Arlo filmed all the time. It all became a routine—a glorious, living-and-breathing skating routine. It got so I didn't even notice the camera anymore. It also got so I didn't think about Dad being there. I just took it for granted that he would help me every day.

Dad promised that after I got a little more comfortable with my ollie, he'd teach me to kickflip. If I could master that, I'd be a real skater.

"Everyone who skates is a real skater," Dad reminded me when he overheard me saying that to Arlo one day.

"I know, I know," I said. I was starting to believe it. It seemed like I'd finally left the Skate Park Disaster behind. I still wanted to get to the kickflip though. And there was something else.

"Dad, what about dropping in?" I asked. We were all over at Gus's. Arlo and I were painting another room while Gus and Dad were tearing out a closet to turn it into another bathroom. "When can I learn how to do that?"

"How about today?"

"At the Silver Bowl?"

Dad laughed. "Well, that's a little steep to start out on. How about we try at the skate park first?"

So after we cleaned up, we headed over.

Dad led me to a mellow bank. I'd skated over it plenty of times, but this time I was going to start at the flat part on top and pretend to drop in, even though the bank was so low the ground would almost immediately rise up to catch me. Dad demonstrated how to lever the board down, holding it with your toes on the back. He leaned forward and slammed his wheels down, then glided away. "Your turn!" he called as he skated back.

I set myself up, my board hovering in the air, then pressed down on my board... and fell backward. "You have to make sure your shoulders go down first," Dad said. He demonstrated again, and I saw it: You had to lean into a drop. Standing too straight was what had made me fall. This time I pressed my board down with my front foot and leaned forward. The ground met my wheels with a satisfying *thrum*.

"Okay, that's good," Dad said after I did it again.

"What's the next step?" I figured it'd be like the ollie or the shuvit: Dad would break it down into sections for me, then we'd try to put the whole thing together, and then I'd keep practicing till I got it.

But he shook his head. "The next step is doing it. You don't want to psych yourself out by thinking about it too much. Just go for it. You'll get it, don't worry." He laughed and added, "And if you don't, you know how to fall."

"Oh. Okay." I tried to pretend I was as confident as he was as we skated over to the half-pipe. I climbed up the bank. I studied the tip of my board, trying not to notice how far down the bottom of the pipe was, trying not to remember the last time I tried to drop in.

It didn't work. When I closed my eyes to push the thought away, it only made it more vivid in my mind: the ground meeting my elbow, my arm bent wrong, my knee bleeding. Turns out I hadn't left the Skate Park Disaster behind after all.

"Daf?"

I opened my eyes. Dad stood at the bottom of the half-pipe, nodding like this was going to happen, no question. And then I realized something: He was right. I knew how to fall. I was no longer a ten-year-old kid with no idea what she was doing. More importantly, I wasn't alone. Dad was here for me, and Arlo and Gus too. If it didn't work, I would fall, and it wouldn't be that big a deal. For the first time in a long time, I invoked the old chant, whispering it under my breath: *Ollie, nollie, kickflip, shuvit. Backside, frontside, fakie, grind.*

Then I leaned forward and dropped in.

Swooooop. My stomach felt like it was flying up out of my body and into the air as I rolled back up the other side.

Arlo and Gus whooped from the sidelines. Dad clapped his hands. "Yes! Perfect!"

I grinned as I rolled back and forth. "Can I do it again?" I called over.

"You better!"

I dropped in so many times that the fear completely faded. I only thought about the rush as my board hit the concrete. After a while, Dad and Gus said they had to go home and get some more work done on the house, but Arlo and I decided to stay. He wanted to head back over to the mellow banks so he could practice skating alongside me while holding his camera. "I have to get where I can hold it really steady," he said.

It was pretty interesting watching Arlo crouch down, rolling alongside me while angling his camera up and filming while he was moving. At first he kept falling or going off in the wrong direction, but then he started getting the hang of it, and I started looking back at the half-pipe. I wanted to feel that swoop in my stomach again. But a bunch of guys were over there now.

Arlo saw me looking. "You want to go back over?" I shrugged, and Arlo rolled his eyes. "You've already proved yourself a million times over."

"It's okay. Maybe later."

"Nope. Now you've convinced me." He tugged on the camera strap around his neck. "You *have* to go over there. It's not about how good you are. It's about not caring what those guys think. Come on." He skated over to the ramp, and before I could stop him, he called up to the other skaters, "Hey! Can my friend have a turn? I need to film her for a project."

Four of the guys shrugged like they didn't care one way or the other, but the fifth guy said, "Sure, come on up."

I couldn't back out after that. I climbed to the top of the ramp, Arlo right behind me. I recognized their tricks: a lot of rock 'n' rolls, ollies, and 50-50s, all really cool but nothing super amazing. One of them seemed uncomfortable on his board, and I could hear Dad's voice in my head: "He's too conscious of where his feet end and his board starts." But it wasn't like the Silver Bowl Sesh, where one person went and everyone watched. The ramp was wide enough that people just dropped in whenever it was clear. No one was going to politely nod his head at me and tell me to take my turn.

I had to take it myself.

I looked over at Arlo peering through his viewfinder at the skaters. Dad told me not to psych myself out by thinking about it too much, but that's exactly what I was doing. I edged myself over so I was a little farther away from the guy already skating and set my tail on the coping, then *whoosh*, I dropped in! I distantly heard Arlo call "Niiice!" as I rolled up the other side and back down. At the bottom, I went for an ollie.

It was a total fail.

The falling lessons Dad gave me came in handy because I didn't even think about it: I scrambled back to my feet, my board rolling up and down the side of the ramp on its own in a pathetic little slide. I waited for the laughter. I waited for them to tell me to go home.

"Good one! Shake it off!"

"Yeah, you'll land it next time."

I looked up. A couple of the guys at the top of the half-pipe had been watching. They moved aside as I came back up like they assumed I'd try again. And I did.

I pumped to get my speed up and headed to the top. I felt the satisfying *click* of my board against the coping, then fakie rocked.

When I got back to the top, one of the guys said, "Not bad for a girl."

"Aw, that's bull," the other one said. "She's better than you, and you know it."

"True dat," the first guy said. He laughed and held out his fist. I awkwardly bumped his knuckles with mine and turned to Arlo. "You okay if I keep going?"

"Sure," he said. "If these guys don't mind being filmed too."

"Just tag us if you post it anywhere," said the one who'd stuck up for me. Arlo pulled out his phone so he could get their info, but I kept my eyes on the half-pipe. I couldn't wait to drop in again.

We stayed at the skate park until dark.

19

On Tuesday it was time for another Silver Sesh, but it wasn't awkward like that first time. Everyone knew Dad was teaching me stuff, and they'd all told me stories of their early days as skaters, encouraging me.

But tonight I was going to drop in.

I stood holding my board on the deck of the bowl, watching. Everyone had their own style. Isaiah made every trick seem effortless, and Dad glided easily into whatever he was doing. Gus had this way of throwing his body into a trick so you didn't think he was going to make whatever he was trying to do.... But then he did. I wondered what my style was, or if I even had one yet.

Dad popped up next to me, panting a little. "So? You ready to show 'em what you got?"

I nodded, but I didn't feel ready. It wasn't only that this was steeper than the half-pipe at the skate park. I looked around. The bowl was empty. Everyone was waiting for me. I wanted to tell them to stop watching, but that would be silly. We were all here to watch each other. "Okay," I muttered to myself. I could do this. I put my tail on the coping. I leaned my right shoulder forward, and I dropped in.

I crouched low as my board met the bottom of the bowl. I was concentrating so hard on leaning left so I could carve out the other side and come back down that it took me a second to understand what I was hearing: the sound of skateboards pounding on the deck. For *me*!

I circled the bowl till my nerves calmed down a little, and then I came up the side and landed by Dad. Someone else dropped in, but I couldn't watch because Arlo's camera was in my face. "Stop!" I said, laughing. "Get away."

"How does it feel to drop in for the first time at the

famed Silver Bowl Sesh, also known as the Old Man Skate Sesh?"

"Hey!" Gus called out. "Be gentle with us, kid!"

Arlo was smiling behind his camera. "Any words for our fans?"

"No comment." I put my hands in front of my face, pretending that Arlo was paparazzi.

"Come on, Daphne," Arlo said in his regular voice. "A reaction shot would really be good for the film."

He wanted a reaction? I stepped right up to the camera and shoved my face into the lens. "How does it feel? Awesome! There. Is that good enough for you?"

Arlo laughed and lowered the camera. "That was perfect."

Afterward, when it was time for all the guys to sit around and drink beer or, in Dad's case, bubbly water, Gus said, "You're one of us now, Daphne. You and Arlo have to stay and hang out with the old folks this time." I grinned, still elated about dropping in, and took the chair next to Dad. Arlo sat on my other side.

Everyone started talking about me: Diego thought

it was so cool that Dad was teaching me how to skate and said he needed to bring his kids one of these times. Rusty said I learned so quickly that maybe she should give it another try. Tyler said I had a natural talent. Isaiah told me and Arlo that we should hang with him at the skate park sometime. It was kind of nice, but it was also a little too much. I turned to Gus to change the subject. "Dad says you guys used to go on epic skate-camping trips."

"Yeah?" Isaiah asked. "Sounds cool. Let's bring back the tradition!"

"You told her about those trips?" Gus asked. When Dad nodded, Gus cleared his throat. "We were a lot younger back then." He raised his eyebrows at Dad. "A little wild."

I scanned Dad's face. I was pretty sure I knew what Gus was getting at. "I was drinking a lot," Dad admitted. "But in a way those trips with you were one of the more wholesome aspects of my life at the time."

"Yeah." Gus seemed to relax once Dad said that. He turned to Isaiah. "It was when Joe lived in L.A., so we'd usually head out into the desert, with as many of us as we could round up for a weekend or a week or however long people could get away for. We'd pick a skate park, head toward it, and find a place to camp along the way. Those desert landscapes"—Gus whistled—"so beautiful. A couple of times we found natural hot springs. One night there was this incredible meteor shower."

"I remember that," Dad said, leaning back in his chair and looking up at the sky like he could see it right then. "I never saw so many shooting stars at once."

I nudged Arlo. "Have you ever been camping?"

He snorted. "Of course. Mom and I used to do it all the time with…" He looked at Gus. "We went on a bunch of fishing trips, so we camped at different lakes and stuff."

Gus's eyes crinkled. I was pretty sure he knew Arlo was referring to one of Rusty's old boyfriends. "There's nothing like sleeping under the stars," he said.

"We should do it again." Dad said it quietly at first, as if he was thinking out loud, but then he repeated himself, looking around the circle at Gus, Arlo, me, Isaiah, Diego, Tyler, and Rusty. "We should go on another road trip. Maybe go north this time."

"There are lots of parks in Portland and Seattle," Tyler agreed.

"Are you guys serious?" Diego asked. "Because I would totally ask for time off work if you were."

"I'm definitely serious!" Dad said. "I'd like to do one of those trips sober, to be honest. And Daphne here has never been camping!" His voice rose in outrage.

Tyler pounded his fist on the table. "Now *that's* a crime! We have to fix it."

"I know, right?" Dad said.

Suddenly everyone was leaning over Gus's phone, looking at a map and talking about places they've always wanted to go. Rusty rolled her eyes and went inside. When she came back, she waved around an old-fashioned paper map. "This is what you need if you're going to plan a camping trip. Head anywhere there's water, that's what we used to do, right, Ar?" She ruffled Arlo's hair. He dodged his head away from her, but he smiled.

"Those trips were pretty fun," he admitted to me. "I never got into the fishing part so much, but swimming and hiking around was cool."

Dad leaned over the table looking at the map with everyone else. I tugged on the back of his T-shirt. "Wait, so are we really doing this?"

Dad straightened and looked at me. "You really want to hang out in a van with a bunch of old, smelly skater dudes?"

"Hey," said Rusty. "I'm going too! We'll make sure the place doesn't get too stinky, right, Daf?"

I grinned at her. "Yes!" I'd always wanted to go camping. And skating too? It sounded like heaven. "Can we have s'mores?" I asked. "And roast hot dogs on a stick and..." I tried to think of all the other things Sam had told me she did at her summer camps. "Sing songs around the campfire?"

"And tell ghost stories!" Arlo put in.

"Don't forget skating," Gus added.

"Every chance we get!" I said.

Everyone started putting in their two cents about what we should do and where we should go. "Part of the fun of a skate trip is not knowing exactly where you're going," Isaiah objected as Gus jotted down a list of places we might want to go. Tyler said it was good to have at least a few ideas. Then everyone brought out their phones to check their calendars. It was hard to find days when no one had another commitment to their families or work, but they finally found five days in August that worked for everyone.

As they all bent over their phones to enter the dates, Dad pulled me aside. "Daf, I need to ask your mom if this is okay. I should have thought of that before we started planning, but I got a little carried away." He flashed his dimple at me, but it faded quickly. "Also, when I said before that I couldn't believe you'd never been camping, I didn't mean it was your mom's fault or anything. I meant *I* should have been there to take you camping, that's all."

"It's okay, Dad." I was so excited about this trip, nothing could bother me. "And don't worry. Mom's going to be fine with it." She had to be. There was no way I was going to miss a skate-camping trip!

Dad had a worried frown on his face as we walked back to his house. When we got inside, he said, "Let your mom know I need to talk to her when you text her tonight, okay? I think we better talk, not text."

"I'll do it right now," I told him. I had just enough time to catch her before she started work. Dad went to the kitchen, and I plopped onto the couch.

> **Hi Mom! Got a minute?**

> I'm about to leave for the set. How's things? Your dad found a job yet? 😬

I paused, remembering how miserable I was a couple of weeks ago. We still texted or video chatted every day, but Mom was so busy that it was mostly quick updates. She'd tell me a funny story about something that had happened on set, and I'd tell her about my tourist adventures with Grandma Kate or helping Gus and Arlo fix up the house.

I hadn't mentioned skating much.

At first it was because I wasn't sure it was going to stick. And then when Dad and I started skating together, I was afraid she'd say something that would mess with the way we were getting along. If I told her now, she'd think it was strange that I hadn't mentioned it.

> **No, but he got a second interview.**

I'd told Mom about his job hunt a while back, and she kept asking about it. Now I felt bad every time I told her he still didn't have a job—like I was letting Dad down somehow. Before she could say anything else about that, I typed quickly.

> **We're going camping! Dad wants to talk to you to make sure it's OK. Can you call us when you're done with work today?**

Ugh, camping! You know what that means, don't you? Bugs, dirt, sleeping on the hard ground, and burnt hot dogs. 😫 That's what I remember from the times your dad got me to go with him.

Please Mom? I want to go!

Of course, Babygirl. It's good timing. I have something I need to talk to him about too. Something exciting! 😏 I'll call in the AM your time, OK? For now, gtg. Love you so so so much! 😍

Love you Mom! 💜

Dad was sitting at the kitchen table, staring at his laptop screen.

"Mom says she'll call you tomorrow morning," I told him.

He nodded slowly and lifted his gaze from his computer.

"Dad, are you okay?" His eyes seemed distant, like

202

he wasn't actually seeing me. I froze. Was something bad about to happen again?

But he kept nodding. "I'm okay. I—I got a job." He blinked, and his eyes came back into focus. "I can't believe it. I actually got a job."

"You did? Dad, that's great!"

He shut his laptop and stood up. "Thanks. It is great, isn't it? Wow! You have no idea how relieved I am." He beamed at me. "This summer is turning out to be the best ever."

"Yeah." I started to flash a matching smile back at him, when I thought of something. "Wait. You can still go on the skate trip, right?"

Dad frowned, then nodded. "I'm sure I can tell them I already had this planned. And it's only five days. Should be fine."

20

The next morning after breakfast, Dad and I sat in the kitchen with a bunch of tools on the table and my board lying wheels up in front of us. Dad said skaters should know how to maintain their boards and make adjustments. He had me wiggle the truck bolts. "See how that one's a little loose?" He handed me a wrench. "See if you can tighten it."

I had just gotten the wrench on the bolt when my phone rang. I glanced over at the screen. "It's Mom."

Dad got the same nervous frown he'd had last night. "You talk to her first," he said.

"Hi, Mom!"

"Hi, honey! Listen, I don't have much time," Mom said. She was saying something about needing to watch some rushes, but Dad was distracting me. He was so jittery! He'd pushed his chair back and was standing in front of the fridge. He opened it, shut it, then paced over to the sink, then sat down again. I turned away and looked out the sliding glass door to the backyard. "Mom," I interrupted whatever she'd been saying. "Did you think about the camping trip? It's okay if I go, isn't it? Dad wants to talk to you to make sure."

"Oh, right. Sure, put him on. But then I need to talk to you again, all right? I have something to te-e-ell you!" She sang out the last words.

I handed my phone to Dad.

"Hey, Edy. Sorry, Eden!" He cleared his throat. I hadn't realized he'd be so nervous with Mom. Did he really think she wasn't going to let me go? She'd basically already said yes. I hated watching the way he pulled his hair while he talked to her. It was making *me* nervous. I went to my room, but it took so long that I poked my head out.

"That's not what we talked about." Dad's voice sounded tight, angry even. I popped back into my room. They were arguing.

A few minutes later Dad came in and handed me the phone. I lifted my eyebrows to ask, *Did she say the skate trip was okay?* Dad shot me a quick smile that didn't go to his eyes. "Just talk to her." He left.

That didn't seem good. I lifted the phone to my ear. "Hi, Mom."

"Daphne." Uh-oh. I could tell by her voice something was wrong. "You didn't tell me this was a skate trip."

"Um, yeah." Was that what Dad's expression was about? Was Mom mad at him for letting me skate?

Silence and then a sigh. "Honey, your dad doesn't have a lot of practice at...well, being a dad. Skating is what he loves, and he's always had a hard time seeing that not everyone feels the same about it." Another pause. "You haven't skated in years. Do you even like it? I don't want you to let your dad pressure you into this. He's supposed to be there for *you* while you're there, not going off on some buddy trip with his friends, making you tag along."

"Mom! No!" Relief fluttered in my chest and made it easy to tell the truth. She wasn't going to say no, she just had to make sure I was okay with it. "I want to go! I want to skate! I've been having fun with it!"

"All right," she said with a little laugh. "Clearly I read that wrong! And God knows you're never going to get to sleep under the stars with me, so yes, you can go on this skate trip."

"Yay! Thanks, Mom!"

"Not so fast. I'm going to need you to promise me three things."

"Okay."

"One, you still have to text me every day like we have been, and two, you have to wear a helmet."

"Of course," I said. "What else?"

"I need to make sure you know what to do if your dad goes off the rails while you're away from your grandparents."

"Off the rails?"

"You know. If he drinks."

"Mom! It's fine. He's been fine." I hadn't told her about the night I called Grandma Kate.

"He better be fine! But still, you need to know what to do in an emergency, and if your dad starts drinking, that's an emergency. So you can still call your grandparents, but while you're on that trip, Gus is the person to talk to. I trust Gus to take good care of you."

"You know Gus?"

Mom laughed. "Of course I know Gus! He's been your dad's best friend since they were kids. We all used to hang out, you know."

I tried to picture Mom like Rusty, cheering on a younger Dad as he skated. I couldn't. "Mom?"

"Yes, honey?"

I had to ask. "You're not mad, are you? That I'm skating?"

"No, I'm not mad. A little surprised you didn't tell me, that's all."

"Yeah. Sorry." She obviously didn't love the idea, but at least she wasn't telling me not to.

"Now, are you ready for my news?"

"Sure!"

"You're coming to Prague!" Mom squealed.

"I'm coming to Prague?" I tried to match her excitement, but I couldn't quite do it.

"Yes! I finally did it! I asked one of the producers if you could visit, and it turns out it fits in perfect with my shooting schedule—the weather hasn't been co-operating this week, so the director has to delay my final scenes so she can catch up. It means I'll have a couple of days off! It's not much time, but I don't care! I miss my Babygirl!"

She chattered on, but I couldn't focus on what she was saying. It was odd. I'd begged her for this trip, and now it was finally going to happen. I thought I would feel more excited. Instead, that desperate need to leave seemed far away. All I could think about now was that going to Prague meant time away from my grandparents. It meant time away from skating. Most importantly, it meant time away from Dad.

It wasn't that I didn't still miss Mom—I did! I'd never been away from her for so long. But it felt like Dad and I were in the middle of something right now. Something good. What if things were different when I came back?

"Dad said he was okay with it?" I interrupted Mom saying something about a museum she wanted to take me to.

"Yes, of course. I told him how important this was to you, that it's a once-in-a-lifetime opportunity." I thought of his tight smile when he handed me the phone. He didn't want me to go.

I didn't want me to go.

But I had to. I'd begged Mom for this. She hadn't wanted to ask for any favors, but she went ahead and did it, for me. How could I tell her no?

"I have it all planned," Mom was going on. "You'll fly in on Sunday, spend a few days on set with me, and then we'll go explore the city! I can't wait to introduce you to everyone! Aren't you excited?"

"Yeah. Thanks, Mom." I tried to sound like I meant it.

There was a second of silence on the other end. "Daphne, is everything okay?"

"Yes!" I repeated, forcing more enthusiasm into my voice. Mom knew me too well. "When do I come?"

"The second week in August," Mom said. "It'll be here before you know it!"

"The second week in August?" I repeated, my heart sinking. "But that's—" I closed my eyes. "That's when we're going on the skate trip."

"Oh." The line went so quiet I wasn't sure if Mom was still there. Finally, she said, "You'll just have to go camping another time. This is more important. This is *Prague*, honey!" She seemed so sure that this was what I still wanted.

I stared out the window of my bedroom. A few weeks ago it was what I wanted! But now I wanted to stay and skate with Dad. I wanted—no, I *needed*—to go on that skate trip. How could I explain to Mom how much it meant to me without hurting her feelings? "It's just, it took everyone a while to find a date that worked. There's a bunch of us going. We can't reschedule."

"So you're saying no? To Prague? After all the times you begged me to come?"

"Can I come a different week?"

Mom let out a heavy sigh. "No, honey. That's the only week that works for me."

I bit my lip. I'd never turned Mom down for anything before. I couldn't quite say that I didn't want to come.

"Fine," she said flatly. "Clearly this trip with your dad is important. I'll cancel the ticket reservation."

I hated having Mom mad at me. "I'm really sorry."

Maybe Mom heard the wobble in my voice, because this time she managed to sound halfway convincing. "It's all right, sweetie! You go on your camping trip. We'll see each other before you know it anyway!" There was a muffled sound of voices in the background. "Listen, I better go. We'll talk soon, Babygirl!"

"Thanks, Mom," I said. "Love you."

"Love you!"

We hung up, but I didn't feel great.

I walked back to the kitchen, where Dad was still

sitting at the table, twirling a wrench between his fingers. He dropped it with a clunk when I came in. "Everything okay?"

"Yeah." I slumped into my chair.

"I gotta admit, I'm a little surprised, Daf."

I looked up at him. He was running his hand through his hair that way he did when he was nervous. "About what?"

"Your mom said you begged her to go. I thought...I thought we were getting along."

"We are." I could feel my face getting hot. Did he know I'd been planning to leave this whole time?

"I mean, I guess I get it," Dad said. "A trip to Prague would be hard for anyone to pass up. And hey, it's only a few days. When you get back, we can pick up right where we left off." He picked up the wrench and watched it twirl in his fingers. "I'm disappointed to lose even that much time with you, but like I said, I get it."

"Dad." I leaned back in my chair, understanding dawning. "I'm not going."

"You're not?" He wiped the palm of his hand over his face like he didn't know what to say. "How come?"

"It's the same week as the skate trip," I said. "I told Mom it wasn't going to work."

"You did?"

I nodded.

"Well, that's just...great!" A huge smile spread over Dad's face. "I mean, I wish you could go to Prague, but—"

"It's okay." A matching smile spread over my face. It had been hard, but I was glad I said no to Mom. "Movie sets are kind of boring, actually." I looked down at the table. "Can we go back to the maintenance lesson?"

"Sure." He handed me the wrench. "And then a skate sesh?"

"Perfect."

21

The next day, Dad took me to REI to buy camping supplies. He had most of the gear we needed, but he bought me a warm sleeping bag and a little tent. "You can sleep out in the open with us, but sometimes it's nice to have a place to escape to, especially for, you know, a girl. You're going to be hanging out with a lot of guys, Daf. I'm not going to lie, they can be a little rough around the edges sometimes." I laughed, but I was glad he thought of it. I was wondering where I would change my clothes.

Later Arlo came over, and I showed him my new stuff. When I told him I had no idea how to set up a tent, he insisted we do a trial run. After we got it set up in the middle of the living room, I walked all around it, admiring the bright blue nylon dome.

Arlo held up the rain fly. "You might need this. It rains a lot up there. Should we put it on?"

"Nah." Dad had insisted on getting a tent with a roof made of netting. "I want to be able to see the stars!"

When Dad walked in, Arlo and I were lying in the tent, looking up through the netting at the top. "What's this?" he said, crouching down to peek in the door.

"We're practicing our stargazing," I said. "Want to try?"

He crawled in and managed to squeeze between me and Arlo. "This is definitely not a three-person tent," Arlo said.

"You know *you're* not sleeping in this tent with Daphne, right?"

"Dad! That's so rude!" I elbowed him in the ribs.

"I got you this tent so you could have privacy." He settled back with a sigh. "But it is a pretty sweet setup."

We all lay there, looking up at the ceiling through the tent.

"I can't wait," I whispered.

That night, I stacked my new gear neatly in my

bedroom closet. I kept opening the door to admire it, counting down the days to when I could pack it into the van we were renting so we could all drive together.

On the morning of his first day at his new job, Dad couldn't find his keys *or* his phone. "You'll be fine," I told him, fishing his car keys out of his coat pocket and putting them in his hand. I pointed to his phone on the kitchen table. "And don't worry about me being on my own."

Over the next week, I hung out with my grandparents a lot. Dad was so tired after work we weren't skating together as much, but I wasn't too worried about it. Arlo and I went to the skate park pretty much every day, and besides, Dad's new boss had given him the okay for the time off. We'd have tons of time together during the skate trip. I wasn't the only one excited about it either: At the Silver Sesh, it was all any of us could talk about. We were all set to leave on Saturday.

On Thursday, Rusty and Gus cooked a huge batch of chili, and Arlo told me we were invited to eat with them.

"We can go, right?" I asked Dad when he got home from work. "I already told them we would."

"What?" He was standing in the kitchen, staring into space. "Oh yeah. Sure."

As soon as we got next door, Dad said he needed to find Gus, and I went outside to join Arlo skating in the bowl.

A little while later, Dad poked his head up over the edge of the bowl. "Hey, Daf," he called. "Can you come down for a sec?"

Arlo and I both climbed down the ladder. Dad motioned me over to the bench below the bowl, and Arlo went inside to see if they needed help with dinner. Dad flashed a smile at me, but it seemed forced. He ran his hands up and down his legs. I thought he'd gotten over being nervous around me. "It's fine, Dad," I reassured him. "What's up?"

"Well," he said. "It, ah. . . ." He let out a long sigh. "Work's going pretty well, you know? They seem to like me."

"That's great, Dad."

"Yeah. That's what I wanted to talk to you about. One of the guys I work with has to have some unexpected surgery. He's going to be out for a week. They said if I fill in for him, they'll bump me up to the next pay level, and I want to do it."

"Great!" I leaned back against the bench and inhaled the spicy, delicious smell wafting out of the house. I was looking forward to dinner.

"Yeah." He tugged on his hat brim. "But it means I can't go on the trip."

I laughed, sure I hadn't heard him right. "What?"

Dad cleared his throat. "I, uh, can't go on the skate trip," he repeated.

"Dad." I straightened up slowly. "That's not funny."

"I'm serious. I'm really sorry, Daf. I'm going to take them up on their offer."

I stared at him in disbelief. "Dad, no. You said they told you it was okay to go."

"I know." He pulled at his hat again. "But I could really use the extra money."

I still couldn't take it in. "So just like that. The whole thing's off? All our plans?"

"No, no! The trip's still on! I'll need to check in with your mom, but I worked out the camping part with Gus. You've got your little tent, and Rusty will watch out for you if you need any...you know, girl stuff. You should be all set."

"You can't go," I repeated. "But the trip's still on?"

"I wish I could go with you, but I'm trying to do the responsible thing here," Dad pleaded. "I'll make it up to you, I swear. And like I said, you can still go."

I stared at him, blinking over and over, trying not to cry. Some distant part of me knew his words made some kind of sense. I knew how hard he'd worked at getting this job. But I imagined climbing into the van with all the Silver Sesh guys and watching Dad wave to me from the sidewalk as he grew farther and farther away.

The back door snapped open. "Chili's ready!" Rusty sang out. She was wearing giant red pot holders on her hands and carrying a huge orange pot. Gus came right behind her with a stack of bowls and napkins, and Arlo followed with a handful of spoons. "Everything okay?" Gus said, his eyes moving from Dad to me and back to Dad again.

Rusty set the pot on the table. "Come on over, you two," she called. "Let's eat!"

Eating was the last thing I wanted to do, but I couldn't be rude to Rusty. I sprang up from the bench without looking at Dad and sat next to Arlo. Rusty and Gus chatted cheerfully as they passed the food around, but I didn't say a word.

When we all had bowls full of chili sprinkled with cheese and sour cream, Dad flashed his dimple at me. "Daf, it's going to be fine. You've made such incredible progress on your skating. You're ollieing like a superstar— before you know it, you'll have a kickflip down too!"

I stared at him in disbelief. "You think I'm worried about the skating?" My voice was shaking. Didn't he understand what this trip meant to me?

Dad let out a laugh, but his eyes got wide and nervous.

"What's going on?" Arlo asked.

I kept my eyes on the bowl of chili in front of me. "My dad can't go on the trip," I mumbled. "He's going to stay home and work."

Gus cleared his throat. "I know it's a disappointment, Daphne, but we're happy to have you along on the trip, and—"

I knew Gus was trying to help, but he wasn't. He was making it worse. "It's okay. I'm not going either." I didn't know I was going to say it until the words popped out of my mouth, but now I saw how true it was. There was no way I could go without Dad.

"What?" Arlo laughed. "You're not going to leave me with all those guys. I'm not about to be the only kid. You're coming."

I shook my head. I was afraid that if I said another word, I'd burst into tears.

"But this was going to be the end of my movie, our big camping trip touring the skate parks of the Northwest!" Arlo said. "I get that it's disappointing your dad can't come, but obviously he doesn't want to blow his new job." He said it so calmly, like it all made sense.

And it did. Which was why I felt so horrible. I wished I could be a good sport. But I just couldn't. "No," I repeated. "I'm not going."

"Well, that's great," Arlo muttered. "Just because your dad lets you down, it's okay for you to let me down? This isn't the Skate Park Disaster, you know."

I stood up so fast my chair fell. I couldn't believe he brought that up. "Stop *pushing* me!" I said. "If you hate it so much when people push their way into places, why are you doing it to me?"

Arlo stared at me in horror.

Oh no. We both looked at his mom. Rusty was holding her hand over her mouth.

She obviously knew exactly what I was referring to.

When I looked back at Arlo, his mouth was twisted in disgust. He got up from the table and went inside.

"Arlo?" Rusty ran after him. "What was that all about?"

Gus stood up. "I—uh, I better check on them." He followed Rusty.

"Daphne," Dad said. "What's going on?"

I rubbed my elbow and pressed my lips together.

"Come on, Daf," he said. "Talk to me."

"Talk to you?" I hated that he had absolutely no clue why I was so upset. "Fine." But the words wouldn't come out.

Dad waited, not moving.

"It's just," I finally said, my voice shaking. "It feels like this is what you do. You promise me something and then you let me down."

"Daf, what are you talking about?"

I let out a sharp laugh. "The skate park, of course."

"Skate park?" Dad blinked. "What skate park?"

"You called me on my tenth birthday? You promised me you'd meet me there. You said you'd teach me to ollie!"

He shook his head. "I don't remember."

"You don't remember?" I stared at him in disbelief. "I lied to Mom and went by myself. I waited and waited." I couldn't stand the blankness on his face. "You never came. *I broke my arm when I tried to drop in!*" I shouted.

His eyes darkened with shock. "That was from a skating fall?"

"Yes. And every time you called me, I waited for you to explain why you didn't show up. But you never did." I clutched my elbow, breathing hard. How could he sit there like he had no idea how much he'd hurt me? I needed to hurt him back. "You know what?" I bent down and picked up my board. "Whatever. I don't even care about the skating trip. I'm going to Prague."

He hunched over as if I'd physically punched him. Good. Let him know how it feels.

Out on the sidewalk I pulled out my phone. Why did I ever think staying with Dad would be better than going to see Mom? I texted her with shaking fingers.

> **Guess what? I'm coming to Prague after all!**

Then I skated away as fast as I could.

22

I went to the skate park. The kidney bowl was empty, and I carved around and around, flowing up and down. I wanted to skate out every thought in my brain. The fight with Arlo, the scene I'd caused. Those were bad. But the worst thing, what I really wanted to forget, was that blank look in my dad's eyes. He didn't remember my tenth birthday?

I don't know how long I'd skated before I finally got tired and had to stop. The evening breeze cooled my sweat, and I let out a breath. I didn't feel better, exactly. But I felt calmer. I looked around. The park was empty, except for one guy on the rim of the bowl, watching me.

Dad.

I thought about skating away, leaving him there without a word. It would serve him right. But I didn't really want to.

I climbed up the ramp.

"You were working pretty hard down there." He extended a water bottle.

I nodded warily and took it from him. I was really thirsty.

"Can we talk?"

I shrugged, but when he sat down, his legs dangling in the bowl, I sat next to him. I kicked the heels of my Vans, bouncing them off the concrete.

"You'd just gotten your cast off when I started calling you. You never told me it was from skating." He reached out like he was going to pat my elbow. I flinched away from him.

If you were there, you would have known, I wanted to say, but I just clenched my jaw tight.

"Daf, I don't remember making that promise to you." He took off his hat and scratched his head, then pulled it back down on his head. "When I drink... when I was drinking, I made a lot of promises I didn't keep." He let out a huge sigh. "I know that's no excuse.

Sometimes I look back on the jerky things I did—or didn't do, like come see you at the skate park when I said I would—and it's like that was a different person. Someone I don't like much." He paused. "I'm really sorry I didn't meet you at the skate park."

There was a time when that was all I wanted—for him to acknowledge that he should have been there that day. But it was too late. It didn't help at all. I remembered what he said that day he told me about making amends. "Sorry doesn't cut it," I muttered, and kicked my Vans against the bowl.

Dad let out a short laugh. "Quoting me again." He didn't say anything for a minute. Then he burst out, "Daphne, please don't go to Prague. This is supposed to be my summer with you. Even if you're mad at me, I want you to stay."

I finally lifted my head to look him in the face. "You know what I really don't get?" I asked. "Why are you suddenly so interested in hanging out with me? Why this summer?"

I thought I'd see hurt flash in his eyes again. But the expression on his face was more like...pity? "Daf, are you kidding? Hanging out with you is *all* I've been thinking about."

"That's not true," I said. Did he think I didn't know? "I remember how Mom asked you to start calling me every month, but it was always pretty obvious you didn't actually want to *see* me."

His forehead furrowed. "Where did you get that idea?"

I let out a sharp laugh. "Don't you remember when you first started calling me? I asked you when you were going to visit and you made some excuse." I lowered my voice in imitation of him. "'Uh...I don't think that's going to work right now.' Just because I was ten didn't mean I didn't get that you were blowing me off!"

Dad let out a long sigh. "Look," he said. "I've been trying to avoid saying this, but I think you need to know. I asked your mom if you could come visit me almost two years ago. Right after I got sober."

I stared at him. "Yeah, right." Did he expect me to believe that?

He kept going. "When your mom told me you couldn't come up to see me, I knew she was right. It was too soon into my sobriety. But then I asked if I could come, just for a visit—to see you for a week, a weekend, an hour—I'd take whatever she'd allow. She said no. To all of it."

"That's not true." I said. "Mom wouldn't do that, not without telling me." I was very sure about that. The only reason I was here with Dad now was because she had been desperate and had no one else to turn to. "She's the one who made you start calling me. She thought it would be good for us."

Dad shook his head. "She said I could call you once a month—that's *all* I could do—so that's what I did. Even if you made it clear you didn't want to talk to me—and trust me, you made it very, very clear. Every time you handed the phone back to your mother, I asked her when I could see you, but she kept putting me off. That's why this job is so important to me." He clenched his fists together on his knees and then let them go. "Look. I'm not proud of it, but I let my parents bail me out a lot over the years. They even offered to pay child support, but your mom said that was my job, not theirs."

I stared at him. Mom wouldn't have stopped my grandparents from helping us. Would she?

"The thing is, she was absolutely right. I should be able to help take care of you on my own. I deserved to be tested. But even after two years of sobriety, your mom kept saying I couldn't see you. Until this summer."

"No. You're lying."

He just looked at me, the pity still in his eyes. "I'm sorry, Daf. I don't know what else to tell you. It's the truth, I swear."

I scrambled to my feet and backed away from him. I suddenly remembered the way he said he'd been hoping Mom would get the movie part. Those looks he and Grandma kept exchanging. My bedroom, all painted and ready for me. And the way he was so nervous when I first got there.

"I don't believe you," I insisted. But actually, I wasn't sure.

Dad stood up. "Daf, let's go home, okay? We'll pick this up tomorrow. I'm just... totally exhausted."

He did look terrible. I hesitated, then gave a quick nod.

We skated home, me right behind him.

Usually when I skated, all my focus homed in on my board, and I could forget everything else that was going on.

But tonight it didn't work.

I couldn't forget anything.

When we got home, I went to my bedroom, closed the door, and called the only person I could trust to be honest about this.

"Is it true?"

"Daphne? Is that you?"

"Is it true that my dad's been trying to see me for two years, and my mom wouldn't let him?"

Silence.

"Grandma?"

I heard her sigh. "Yes, dear. It's true."

I tried to blink away the sting of tears. I blinked over and over. It didn't help.

"He told me not to tell you. He didn't want to create problems with your mother," Grandma said. Tears ran down my cheeks faster than I could smear them away with my T-shirt sleeve. "Daphne? Are you all right?"

I let out a shaky breath, but I couldn't get any words out.

"Would you like to come and stay with us tonight, honey?"

I thought of the text I'd sent Mom earlier that she still hadn't answered. When Dad had told me he was bailing on the trip, I figured I could at least go to

Prague. Now Mom was the last person I wanted to see. And it would be a relief to be away from Dad.

"Yes, please," I told Grandma in a small voice.

A few minutes later I was sitting on the edge of my bed when Dad poked his head in my room. "Everything okay?"

I tried to channel the Cold Fish, but I couldn't find it anywhere. I kept my eyes on my skateboard, which I was rolling back and forth over the floor with my feet. The grip tape was starting to peel up at the corner. I rubbed it with the toe of my Vans, trying to make it stick back down. "I'm going to stay with Grandma and Grandpa tonight."

"Oh." Dad nodded, and his face looked somehow even more tired than before. "Okay. Sure."

As if on cue, a car horn beeped out front. I stood up. I slung my backpack over one shoulder and toed my board into my hand.

I'd hoped it would feel satisfying to leave.

But it just felt bad.

Everything felt bad.

I climbed into Grandma's car, and she got out and talked to him. I didn't want to know what they were saying. He was probably telling her how awful I was, how I was a spoiled brat who didn't understand he had to work for a living, and how I ruined his best friend's dinner.

Arlo. The conversation with my dad had pushed Arlo from my mind, but now my cheeks got hot when I remembered the look on his face as he pushed away from the table. I pulled out my phone and sent him a text: **Sorry.** It wasn't enough, but it was all I could manage right then.

"Ready?" Grandma asked with a too-bright smile. I shoved my phone into my pocket and nodded, but I couldn't manage to smile back. She reached out and squeezed my hand. "Everything's going to be fine, sweetheart."

It was such a nice, grandmotherly thing to say. I wanted to believe her.

But I didn't.

23

My grandparents acted like there was nothing they'd rather do than hang out with me all day. The next morning, Grandpa made pancakes for breakfast, and later Grandma took me out for a mani-pedi. We took Lady for a walk and played cards.

I tried to enjoy it. I appreciated them trying so hard. But I couldn't stop thinking the same things over and over. It was like my brain was back at the skate park, carving out the bowl, around and around in circles.

How could Mom not tell me Dad wanted to see me? Didn't she realize how much I missed him?

And Dad. I could hardly absorb what he'd told me. Knowing that he'd been trying to see me and that he'd apologized for not showing up to the skate park definitely changed things. And of course I understood his new job was important. But I kept thinking he could have made something happen so he could still go.

No matter how much I tried to tell myself the situation was different, it felt like the Skate Park Disaster all over again. Like I should have known better than to believe Dad would come through with what he promised. At least Mom kept her promise to let me come to Prague.

But Mom had let me down too.

And now I wasn't going anywhere. I wished I could talk to Arlo. I'd texted him twice more. While I was waiting for Grandma to get ready—we were going to the grocery store—I picked up my phone to see whether he'd responded yet.

I did have a text. But it was from Mom, finally answering yesterday's text.

Babygirl, I'm so sorry. 😟
You coming to Prague isn't
going to work. Tickets
would cost a fortune at this
point 🧸

Plus we're trying to make up
time we lost because of the
weather. 🌩 Loooong days!
We're working 15, 16 hours
at a time! ⏰

I threw my phone down on the couch. Of course she said no.

But it wasn't like I would go now.

Not even if she begged me.

Before this summer I knew where I stood with my parents: Dad didn't care about me, and Mom would do anything for me. Now it was all mixed up. I didn't know how I felt.

I picked up my phone again. I thought about telling Mom how much I had missed Dad all those years, how I thought he didn't visit me because he didn't care enough to make an effort. Instead I typed one question: **Why didn't you let Dad see me when he wanted to?**

I hit SEND.

Then I asked my grandparents if I could stay another night. I really, really didn't want to be at Dad's house the next morning.

It was the day of the skate trip.

I couldn't bear watching everyone load up the van and leave without me.

Grandma drove me back to Dad's the next afternoon. The minute Dad opened the door Grandma said she was going to make some coffee and disappeared into the kitchen. *Real subtle, Grandma.*

Dad and I stood in the middle of the living room. "I'm glad you're back," he said.

I couldn't meet his eyes. "I'm not going to Prague."

"I heard." Another pause. "Daf, I'm really sorry, about everything."

"It's fine," I mumbled.

"Maybe we can—"

"I'm going to my room," I broke in.

"Oh." He nodded. "Okay." I could tell he was disappointed, but I couldn't listen to any more apologies right now. I practically ran down the hall.

This wasn't the Cold Fish. This wasn't me trying to show him how little I cared.

I definitely cared.

I just didn't know what to do about it.

I sat on my bed, my arms wrapped around my legs, my knees pulled to my chest. When I first got here, I'd escaped to my room whenever I didn't want to deal with Dad. This was different. *We* were different. So why couldn't I face him? I pressed my forehead to my knees. My mind was racing. I kept thinking about the trip. Everyone was already gone, including Arlo, who probably hated me. I hugged my legs tighter and imagined them all pulling up to a new skate park every day, listening to the sound of wheels whirring over surfaces. *Scrape-slam! Scrape-slam!* It must be heaven.

Wait a minute. I got off my bed and pressed my ear to the window. It wasn't my imagination—I could actually hear the noise. Someone was skating in Gus's bowl!

"Dad?" I called down the hall. In the living room, Grandma was sitting on the couch with him, coffee mug in hand. By the way they both stopped when I walked in, it was obvious they'd been talking about me, but I didn't care. "Who's skating at Gus's?"

"Gus or Arlo, I guess," Dad said.

"But—they're on the trip."

Dad shook his head. "They didn't go."

"They didn't go? Why not?" But as soon as I asked, I knew the answer. Because of me. I'd ruined it for Arlo, just like Dad had ruined it for me.

I didn't make friends easily. At least, not good friends. When I was a little kid, Mom and I moved around so much that I never had time to get close to anyone. Then when I was in fifth grade, Mom declared she was going to do her best to make sure we stayed in one place, or at least not move to a different school district again. I met Sam that year, and even though I'd never had a best friend before, I knew right away that's what she was.

I hadn't known Arlo very long, but it seemed like he might be like that too. All summer, he had been there cracking jokes and encouraging me. The only times he ever acted the least bit unhappy was when he talked about his mom, and instead of being there for him, I'd made everything worse.

I didn't know what to do about Dad, but I was pretty sure I could figure it out with Arlo. "I'm going over there, okay?"

Dad gave me a half smile. "That's probably a good idea."

I knocked on the door, my heart pounding with nervousness. I could still hear someone skating in the bowl, so I wasn't sure if anyone was inside. When no one answered, I knocked louder. I was about to head to the back gate when the door swung open.

"Hey, Daphne. You're back." Was it my imagination, or was Gus's smile less crinkly than usual? Was he mad at me too?

I took a deep breath. "I'm sorry for ruining dinner the other night. I didn't mean to mess anything up—" I broke off. I had planned to say it quickly, get it over with, but something in my throat caught, and I couldn't finish. My eyes got all hot and dry, and I was afraid that if I blinked, tears would come out. I looked down at my Vans. "I'm sorry," I repeated.

I waited for Gus to say something, and when he didn't, I looked up. Rusty had joined him at the door, and Gus put his arm around her shoulders. It gave me a little hope.

"It's okay, Daphne," Gus said. "I get it. You were disappointed with your dad. Trust me, I've been there." He smiled, and this time I got the full crinkly effect.

"Arlo told me how unhappy it made him that I pushed to move in with Gus," Rusty burst out. "So I confessed." She looked up at Gus and laughed. "I'm not going to lie—it was pretty rough there for a minute! But we're good now, right, Gus?"

"Yep. We're solid." Gus smiled down at her.

"And Daphne, you know it's not your fault or Arlo's,

right? I should have been honest, and that was all on me."

I nodded. It made me feel a little better. But my eyes kept going toward the back gate. I could still hear Arlo skating. "Does Arlo hate me?" I asked, my voice small.

"No!" Rusty said. "Just go talk to him. It'll be fine."

I slipped through the back gate. I made my way to the bowl and climbed the ladder.

Arlo was skating.

When he came up for a grind, he glanced up and saw me. His body jerked, and he half fell, half dropped into the bowl. He caught himself fast enough to stay on his board, and he skated around for a while. I thought maybe he was going to ignore me completely. Maybe he would never talk to me again. Then he popped onto the deck right next to me.

"Hi," I said.

"Hi." No smile, no sign that he was at all happy to see me.

"You didn't go on the trip."

He shook his head, his lips pressed together. "Nope."

"Um. Because I didn't go?"

"Partly." The same tight expression on his face.

I realized I'd assumed that all I had to do was show up and, like Rusty said, it would be fine. But clearly cracking a LEGO joke wasn't going to work this time.

I had to fix this. But how? My eyes darted around the bowl as if I could find an answer there. And I did. Because it reminded me of Dad teaching me how to drop in. Don't overthink it, he'd said, just go for it.

"I'm sorry for what I said!" I blurted out. "About you pushing me. I didn't mean to make your mom feel bad."

"She knew right away what you were talking about," Arlo said. "She gave me a hard time for telling you our business."

I stared down at my feet. "Sorry," I murmured again. I felt awful.

"Yeah, well." Arlo shifted on his feet. "My mom also told me I *was* pushing you too hard. She said I should have noticed how upset you were. So . . . I'm sorry too."

I looked up, surprised. "You are?"

"Yeah." He lifted one shoulder. "I just really wanted to go on that trip, you know?"

"Yeah," I said sadly. "Me too."

We both stared into the bowl.

"I know!" Arlo snapped his fingers. "Let's both agree to blame everything on our parents instead of each other."

I laughed. "I love that plan."

"Seriously though, my mom ended up apologizing to me. She didn't realize the whole thing was bugging me so much. She told Gus everything."

"Wow." I looked toward the house. "Things seemed pretty good with them though."

"Yeah. Actually, it was Gus who said we shouldn't go on the skate trip so we could talk it all out. He said we need to be able to be honest with each other if we're going to"—Arlo cleared his throat—"be anything like a family."

I drew in a breath. "Whoa."

"Yeah."

We stared into the bowl again.

"Hey, I thought you were going to Prague," Arlo said.

"Nope. My mom got too busy."

"That's too bad."

"Actually...," I said. "You know how I said I hadn't seen my dad in three years?" Arlo nodded. "Well, it turns out he'd been asking my mom if he could visit me for a while. And she never told me."

Arlo whistled. "That's intense."

"Yeah. I'm pretty mad at my mom right now."

"What about your dad? Everything cool with him?"

I shrugged. "Kind of? Not exactly." I shrugged again. "I don't know!"

Arlo laughed. "That doesn't sound so cool." He strummed his fingers on the nose of his board. "You know, at first I thought it was corny how Gus made a big deal about us having this 'Talk.'" He rolled his eyes. "But it did kind of help."

I sighed. I didn't like talking. Not about stuff like that. But I knew Arlo was right. It was the only answer to the question I'd just been asking myself. I had to talk to Dad. Mom too, I guessed.

Arlo nodded to my empty hands. "You didn't bring your board?" When I shook my head, he said, "Go get it. I'll wait."

That was the thing about Arlo. He knew when to talk and when to skate.

24

I knew I should march into the house and announce to Dad, "We need to talk!"

But when I got home from my mini skate sesh with Arlo, and he said, "Can you handle some more skating?" I told him I could.

It was true, but also, I was glad for an excuse to put off talking. "Where we going?"

"You'll see."

As Dad drove, I tried to figure out which skate park he might be taking me to. I knew there were a few in Oakland, or maybe we'd go to Berkeley or another nearby city. But when he stopped the car, I didn't see a skate park anywhere. We were in a huge commuter-train parking lot under the freeway. Even inside the car I could hear the sound of the rapid transit trains as they pulled in and out of the station on the rails above our heads. "We're taking BART somewhere?"

Dad shook his head, a little smile on his face. "Nope. Grab your board."

We threw down and pushed over toward the edge of the parking lot. I heard the sound of wheels scraping on asphalt before I saw the small group of skaters bombing around.

"This is pretty much where I started out," Dad said. "Street skating—using your surroundings and doing whatever you can think of with them." We watched as a guy near us ollied up onto a stair railing and did a feeble grind down it, which is a combination of a 50-50 and a boardslide.

"I'm totally ready to do that," I joked.

"It'll come sooner than you think probably," Dad said. "You're right at the point where things are going to start falling into place and the tricks are going to come more easily."

"You really think so?" I asked, studying the skater, who was going down the railing again.

"I know so. But let's not worry about that right now. Let's just skate."

At first I was a little nervous being in a new place, but when I looked around, no one was paying the slightest attention to me. *I'm as much of a skater as any of them*, I reminded myself. I started working on getting my ollie up the curb, and Dad sailed off to do his own thing. I was so focused that I didn't realize anyone was watching until a voice behind me said, "Looking good!"

A woman skater gave me a thumbs-up and a big smile. I grinned back, and she skated away.

Arlo and I had watched a couple of movies about women and girl skaters, and Dad had told me about pioneers like Cara-Beth Burnside and Jaime Reyes, but the truth was, I hardly ever saw girls skate in real life. I looked around and realized this woman wasn't the only one here. "Cool," I said. I remembered the girl skaters Grandma and I had seen in San Francisco. Maybe someday I'd be like that, cruising around and inspiring other girls to join in.

Dad circled back to me and jumped off his board. He took off his hat and wiped his sweaty face with the arm of his T-shirt. "Okay if we take a break?" he asked.

I nodded, and we went across the street to a café to get drinks—bubbly water for Dad and boba for me. Then we parked ourselves on a low concrete wall back in the lot to watch people skate.

"So... you and Arlo okay now?" Dad asked.

"Yeah." I nodded. "We're good."

To be honest, it was pretty great, sitting with Dad, tired from skating and watching other skaters, knowing we'd join them again in a bit. It would be easy to leave it at that. But I knew Arlo was right. I needed to talk to Dad. The problem was, I wasn't sure how to start.

In front of us, a guy attempted a kickflip, but his board flew out from under his feet and he fell back on his butt. "Ouch!" Dad and I both said at the same time. We looked at each other and laughed. Dad leaned over and said in my ear, "He never learned how to fall." I laughed again, but it brought back our first skating lesson, when Dad had insisted on teaching me how to fall. It was like that now: It didn't really matter if I didn't say the exact right thing to him. Even if I fell, I knew how.

"So." I bit my lip, gathering my nerve. "What made you want to see me again... you know, a couple years ago?"

He lowered his water, coughing. "What do you mean? I always wanted to see you."

I shot him a look. "Dad."

"I'm serious, Daf. Before I got sober, my life was one big screwup, but there was always a bright spot: the times I got to see you. So, when I got sober for real, you were my top priority. I just had to wait for your mom to be ready to trust me again."

I kept my eyes on the skaters, but I wasn't really paying attention to them anymore. It *sounded* good, what Dad was saying. Like he was only thinking of what was best for me. But something didn't quite ring true. I pushed my straw in and out of the plastic cup, trying to figure out what it was.

I had finally told Dad about the Skate Park Disaster. He'd apologized for it. I should feel better. But I didn't.

And then I understood what the real problem was. It was the number one skating rule Dad taught me: You can't expect to land a trick if you back off at the last minute. You have to fully commit.

It was like that now. I couldn't tell Dad just part of the story. I had to commit.

"I used to think," I said, turning back to the parking lot. It was easier to watch the skaters than to look at him. "When I was a little kid, I thought it was like magic, the way you'd come around when I was missing you. Just when it seemed like you'd forgotten about me, you'd show up! You'd take me to a skate park or the beach or to get a hamburger or whatever. I'd brag about you to my friends the next day, tell them you were the most awesome dad. And I remember wondering, 'How does he always know when I need to see him?' I thought you could read my mind or something."

"Really?" Dad said. He was smiling like I'd said something sweet. He didn't get it.

"Dad." I put my boba down. "It wasn't magic. Why did I have to be *desperate* to see you? It wasn't only my tenth birthday and the Skate Park Disaster. It was all the years before that. I never knew when you'd come around! I had friends who would see their dads for a whole weekend. I only ever got a couple of hours at the most." His smile had faded by now. "I thought it was my fault. That I wasn't important to you." I clutched my elbow.

"No, Daf. I swear it wasn't that," Dad said. "Back then, your mom only let me come around when I was sober, so that's when we did that fun stuff. She was right, of course. The problem was, I wasn't sober too often." He let out a short laugh. "I somehow convinced myself I was doing something good when I didn't come around, that I was making it easier for everyone." He shook his head. "One thing alcoholics are really good at is making excuses for being jerks."

I could feel Dad watching me, but I hugged my elbow close to my body and trained my eyes on a skater sailing off the curb near us. I had to make sure I understood. "So the reason I hardly ever saw you was because of your alcoholism?"

"Yes," Dad said. "It had nothing to do with you and everything to do with me and my problems." He sighed. "Look. I don't expect you to forget those years. They happened, and I'll *always* regret not being in your life more back then. But I've said it before, and I mean it. I want to make amends to you. And not just skating. Everything. What do you think? Can you be okay with that?"

I pressed my lips together. It was true that a huge weight had been lifted when I told him what I'd worried about all these years. But there was something else I had to ask. "You're not going to drink again, are you?"

He winced. "I can't make any promises, Daf. I'm going to do my very best not to drink, but I have to take it one day at a time. That's the way we do it."

It wasn't very comforting.

He nudged me. "You know, it's kind of like skating."

"What do you mean?"

"One of the great things about skating is how it's all about accepting failure and moving on from it. You know how you can try and try to land a trick, but even when you can't, you just keep at it?" I nodded. That I definitely understood. "Well, that's how not drinking is for me. If I ever mess up again, I'm going to keep at it. I'm not going to give up. You think you can live with that?"

"Yes," I said. "I can live with it." And I realized something: I trusted Dad. He wasn't perfect, but who was? The important thing was that I knew he'd be there for me. I let go of my elbow, and it felt like I was letting go of the anger and hurt I'd been holding on to for all these years too.

"Dad, I have one more question."

He turned to me, concern in his eyes.

"Can we skate some more?"

He grinned. "Always."

Later that night I finally got a text from Mom. Her reply was long, with not a single emoji.

Daphne, it's my job to protect you. I hated seeing your disappointment when your dad let you down over and over when you were younger. I knew how much you loved seeing him, so I put up with his flakiness, but that time you broke your arm because you thought he was coming to see you was the last straw. There was no way I was going to give him the chance to hurt you like that again— emotionally OR physically. I was doing what I thought was best for you. And I'm not sorry.

I read it over a few times. The thing about Mom was, she could never admit when she was wrong. She didn't understand how much it hurt me to think Dad didn't want to see me.

I laid my phone on the table by my bed, facedown.

I wasn't ready to answer her.

But the next day, I sat in my bedroom, my skateboard wheels up on my lap, running my hands across all the scratches on the bottom of the deck. I remembered how there were only a few grooves at the beginning of my visit, back when I was texting or call-ing Mom every day and saying how much I hated stay-ing with my dad. I'd had the big Talk with Dad; I might as well have it out with my mom too.

I video called her.

"Babygirl!"

I still wasn't used to her blond hair, but it was good to see her face appear on the screen, despite every-thing. So I had to say it right away, before I lost my nerve: "Mom, you had no right to lie to me!"

She inhaled sharply. "I didn't *lie* to you."

A flash of anger stabbed at my chest. "You never told me Dad wanted to visit me. That's like lying. I thought he was avoiding me."

"Honey." Her voice was soft. "You don't remember how bad it was. How many times he let you down. You were too young."

A lump suddenly formed in my throat and made it hard to talk. But I needed her to understand. "That doesn't mean you get to take him away from me. That wasn't your choice!"

"Daphne." The softness disappeared. "It *was* my choice. I'm your mother. It's my job to keep you safe."

"But—"

"Look. Your dad seems like he's in good shape now, so maybe you can't imagine it. That's because I protected you from the times he was falling-down drunk. When he—" Mom broke off. "Never mind. You don't need to know the details."

I ground my teeth together. "Well, what about when he stopped drinking? Why didn't you give him another chance?"

"I gave him plenty of chances before that, believe me. There was no reason for me to believe him when he said he was sober. I'd heard it before."

So many arguments ran through my head. The same ones I'd been thinking ever since I found out that she'd stopped my dad from seeing me. *You let me think he didn't care. If I had known, maybe I would have asked him about the Skate Park Disaster. Maybe I wouldn't have been so cold to him all those times on the phone.* I sighed. I was pretty sure that no matter how much I argued, I wasn't going to change how Mom looked at the past. But maybe I could change the way she looked at the future.

"Mom. Things are different now. Dad's going to stay in my life. Whatever happens when we're together, it's between him and me."

"Daphne, you're twelve years old. How are you going to handle it if he messes up?"

I thought about Dad telling me he couldn't make any promises that he'd never drink again. I still didn't like not knowing for sure, but I had to live with it. And so did Mom. "If Dad messes up again, you can't protect me from it. And trust me, if it does happen, I'll let him know how I feel."

"I bet you will, Babygirl." Mom laughed. "Okay. I promise not to keep him out of your life anymore." She brushed a finger under her eye.

"Are you crying?" I accused.

"Maybe a little." She laughed again. "It's just, you're growing up! You're becoming a strong young woman, you know that? I miss you."

I smiled. We were back to normal now. "Thanks, Mom. I miss you too."

25

My stay in Oakland was almost over. Dad was working a lot, and while he was gone I hung out with my grandparents or Arlo. When Dad got home from work, we usually headed to the skate park. I was finally getting the kickflip down, at least sometimes. I understood the way I had to flick the board at the top of the ollie so it would do a full 360 spin before I landed on it. The thrill I got whenever I landed it never faded.

But even better than landing a kickflip was hanging out with Dad, skating until we were so tired we had to stop, and then sitting and watching the other skaters till it got dark, sometimes analyzing their tricks, sometimes talking about other stuff.

We spoke a little about the future. I told him next summer I wanted to go to the skate camp Grandma had told me about.

"I'd love for you to do that," Dad said. "As long as your mom is okay with you coming up next summer."

I hadn't told him the details of our conversation, but he knew I'd talked to her. "She'll be okay with it," I assured him.

Dad laughed. "Somehow I believe you."

Arlo's summer class was having a "film festival," where everyone was going to show their final project in a theater at the local high school. Dad and I went, of course.

You wouldn't think you could do a lot in three minutes, but each of the fifteen films we sat through was so different. Some of them had people acting out a scripted story. A couple were more artsy, floating from one image to the next. One even featured LEGO figures as the lead actors. I hit Arlo on the arm and whispered, "Coulda been you!" and he grinned back at me.

Finally, Arlo's movie came on.

I had seen pieces of it as he'd edited it on his computer, but he'd never let me watch it all the way through. I was a little nervous about seeing my face up there on a big screen in a room with a bunch of people, even if it was mostly the other kids' parents. But once it started I forgot about everyone else.

The opening scene was a tiny dot that zoomed in so gradually that it took a while before you could tell it was a girl on top of the quarter-pipe at the skate park, holding her board against her leg, watching a couple of guys do their tricks.

Me.

Somehow, just by the way the camera caught me watching those guys, you could tell I wanted to be a part of what they were doing. Then he cut to us bombing over the bumps in the parking lot. He laid some grinding guitar music over the skate park scenes, but every once in a while the music would stop, and he'd cut in someone talking. At one point Dad was saying, "Try again," then I was trying to ollie, then "try again," all of it over and over. Just when it was getting as frustrating to watch as it was in real life, there was my first tiny ollie! Arlo inserted his own face in there saying, "Rad." The audience laughed.

Another section of quick cuts back and forth had me at the top of the bowl, the nose of my board hovering over it, then it cut to a watching skater saying, "She's got this," and back to me still hesitating, and then someone else saying, "She's got this." When I finally dropped in, Dad let out a whoop in the seat next to me. I elbowed him. "Shhh!" I said, but I was watching my face on the screen. I was grinning, and it was clear I wasn't worrying about belonging anymore. There were a few more shots of me in the park—in one I landed a kickflip—and then it was the last shot: me flowing through the skate park, the camera pulling out till I was a little dot again, like at the beginning.

Everyone clapped at the end, and when Arlo stood up to take a bow as he'd been told to, he pulled me up alongside him. My face heated with embarrassment, but it was nice too. Especially the big smile Dad was throwing at me.

Still, I was glad when the applause stopped and the next movie started. I sat in the dark, marveling at how strange it had been to watch myself up there.

I thought back to the beginning of my visit with Dad and how I'd tried so hard not to admit that I wanted to skate. Somehow my love of skating had gotten all tangled up with my love for Dad, and I thought

I couldn't have one without the other. Dad and I had worked a lot of stuff out, and I was really glad about that. It helped me realize that whether I was a skater or not wasn't up to him, it was up to me. But seeing myself up there on that screen confirmed it, once and for all: I was a skater now for real.

On the Sunday of my last weekend in Oakland, Gus and Rusty hosted another one of their barbecues—a combination goodbye party for me and another showing of Arlo's film because the Silver Sesh guys and my grandparents insisted on seeing it. Afterward, Grandma Kate said, "Maybe you take after your mother after all, huh? You were pretty photogenic up there." I rolled my eyes. It wasn't that bad being in Arlo's movie. But I was way more interested in skating.

I skated the bowl one last time, of course. Diego had brought his two little boys, and I caught them watching me with a familiar look of admiration on their faces. I grinned and asked them when they were going to come skate with us. They got all shy on me, but Diego assured me he was working on it with both of them.

When we sat down to eat, the Silver Sesh guys

started handing around their phones and sharing pictures from the skate trip. "Too bad you couldn't make it to this one, Daphne," Isaiah said. "You definitely gotta come next time. You too, Arlo."

"Next summer for sure," I agreed, the jab of regret not quite as bad as it was.

"About that," Dad said. "I've been thinking. What if we did a quick skate trip Labor Day weekend?"

"I'm in!" said Isaiah.

"Me too," Diego said. "This time I'll bring my kids."

Everyone started talking at once, and it was just like when we planned the original trip. I nudged Dad. "What about work?" I asked in a low voice. "And Mom?" I didn't want to get my hopes up again if it wasn't going to happen.

"Actually"—Dad's dimple poked through his cheek—"I already cleared it with both of them."

Arlo and I grinned at each other. "We're both going this time," I promised. "No matter what."

At the end of the barbecue, I had to say a few goodbyes. The skaters all fist-bumped me and said they couldn't wait to see what I was up to next time I was in town. Rusty and Gus both hugged me, and so did Grandpa Jim.

Grandma Kate squeezed me extra tight, but we'd be seeing each other the next day, so we didn't say goodbye.

But I did have to say goodbye to Arlo.

"I'll see you in a few weeks. And I'm coming up for Thanksgiving too," I told him.

"Cool, I'll be here," he said. "Spending Christmas with my dad this year. Gus told me he'd teach me how to make chicken mole. I'm going to surprise my abuela with it."

I wasn't sure what to do then. Hug? Shake hands? High-five? Arlo solved my problem by grabbing me in a quick one-armed hug and then patting my shoulder twice, bro style. "Bye, Daphne."

"Bye, Arlo."

My flight back to L.A. was the next day. Grandma Kate was taking me to the airport because Dad had to work, but I was almost glad. It seemed easier to say goodbye now and get it over with.

I was taking one last look around my bedroom. I had ended up posting pictures all over the place. One wall was completely devoted to skating: It had a movie poster of *Learning to Skateboard in a Warzone (If You're a Girl)* and some photos torn out from *Thrasher*—I'd finally found a couple of pictures of girl skaters in one issue. I'd claimed one of those old snapshots of Dad skating, and Arlo had given me a still from his movie: me, mid ollie, airborne.

"Your grandma's waiting in the car," Dad said, poking his head in. He saw me looking around. "You can take all this with you if you want."

"Nah," I said. "I like having it here. But...were you serious when you said I can take the board?" I had already laid it on top of my suitcase.

Dad's dimple appeared. "I'll let you in on a little secret: I actually got that for you."

"You did?" I smiled back. I'd sort of thought maybe he had.

"Yep."

"Thanks." I gave the board a little stroke. I wasn't planning on getting rid of my old board, but now I had an extra one for Sam to use if she wanted. It wouldn't really matter if she didn't end up liking skating as much as I did.

But I was going to make her at least try it.

Dad grabbed my suitcase, and we walked out to the car. "Hey," I said, as he loaded my stuff in the trunk. "You think my friend Sam could visit me here next summer?" I knew she and Arlo would get along.

"Sure." Dad nodded, but there was something about his voice that made me peer at him more closely.

"Wait. Dad? You're not crying, are you?" I said. "I'll see you on Labor Day weekend! For the most rad weekend skate trip ever!"

"Sorry," he said, wiping his hand over his eyes. "It's just—it's been great seeing you, Daf. I know I'm not a perfect parent, but I—"

"You know"—I shook my finger at him—"being a parent is a lot like skating. It's all about accepting failure and moving on from it."

"Ha ha, very funny," Dad said. He grabbed me in a big hug. "I'm sure gonna miss you, Daf."

I threw my arms around him and squeezed him tightly. "I'll miss you too, Dad."

I opened the passenger door, but I turned back to Dad.

"Wait. Is everything like skating?"

"Yes," Dad said. "Everything."

I smiled as I slid into the front seat next to Grandma, remembering that first skate lesson with Dad. I'd felt so silly when he taught me how to fall, but it really was true: If you didn't learn that, you'd never know for sure if you could get back up again.

And now I was sure I could.

ACKNOWLEDGMENTS

Huge thanks to my agent, Jennifer Unter, who kept the faith through three books and made it happen in the best possible way. I couldn't do this without you! Thanks also to Jen Nadol for your editorial help and moral support.

Many, many thanks to my editor, Liz Kossnar, who treated Daphne and her story with such loving care. You understood exactly what I was trying to do and pushed me to do it better. It has been such a pleasure to work with an editor who expresses so well what's missing and gives me the freedom to find it my own way!

Thank you also to the fantastic team at Little, Brown Books for Young Readers: editorial assistant Aria Balraj, production editor Jen Graham, art director Sasha Illingworth, designer Gabrielle Chang, marketers Stefanie Hoffman and Shanese Mullins, publicist Shivani Annirood, digital marketer Mara Brashem, manufacturing coordinator Patricia Alvarado, copyeditor Sherri Schmidt, and proofreader Tracy Koontz.

Chris Danger, thank you for making Daphne come alive in your cover drawing! I just love seeing her face peeking out from the spine!

I wouldn't be the writer I am today without the Panama Math and Science Club, my critique group of seven years: Katherine Rothschild, Lisa Moore Ramée, Lydia Steinauer, Rose Haynes, and Stacy Stokes. I hit the jackpot when I met these talented writers and extraordinary friends! It continually amazes me how much I am still learning from each of you and how much we laugh along the way.

Thank you, Lori Wilkinson Baldwin, longtime friend and first reader, eternal supporter, and forever the person I know I can count on.

I appreciate all the children's librarians out there for sharing your love of books with kids, but I'd like to express particular appreciation to my Burger Buddies: Erica Siskind, Michelle Waddy, Annabelle Blackman, and Celia Jackson. Thanks too to all of the Oakland Public Library Children's Services librarians for your support and all around amazing-ness!

A special shout-out to the Ladies: Amalie Hazelton, Caitlin Higginbotham, Erica Siskind (again), and Sabrina

Siskind. Thanks for your moral support and not minding all those times when I said I couldn't get together because I was writing.

Thanks to the skaters from the real-life Silver Bowl Sesh, especially Jeff Bell for his skating expertise and being on call for two years to answer all my questions, and Scott Hewitt for having the skate bowl that inspired much of this story. I also want to express my appreciation for the nonprofit organizations Skate Like a Girl and Skateistan for their good work in supporting young skaters of all genders, in the Bay Area and around the world. Thanks too to the skaters who have bravely documented their skating journeys from the beginning, falls and all, especially @opheliaskatesplymouth, @thepritchardsisters, @ollie_zzolli, and @trinspace.

Over the years, I've attended a lot of writing workshops, classes, and conferences that have been helpful in some way, but there's only one that made me change the way I look at writing novels, and I'd like to thank Nina LaCour's Slow Novel Lab for that!

As a librarian, I love to research, but sometimes you need to talk to a real person to get it straight. Thanks to my fact-checkers: Essi Westerman for sharing her camera knowledge, Brenda Membreño for obscure *Star Wars* characters, Ruby and Stella Hewitt for the lowdown on boba ordering, and D'Arcy Carden for her movie set expertise. Thanks also to Don Rich for taking my dad to AA and making amends in the form of pies, and to Laney Erokan-Footman for helping me with my website text.

Thanks to *all* the Engelfrieds and the many Engelfried-adjacent family members for your support and for being almost as excited as I was when I learned my book was going to be published!

Mom, are you still reading? I know you hate these long acknowledgment sections, so you may have stopped by now, but I can't possibly leave you out. You are the reason so many of your seven kids, fifteen grandkids, and nine great-grandkids (at last count) love books and words and writing. From typing up my early stories to making sure I had a writing desk to showing me how to use *Roget's* and *Bartlett's*, you did so much in laying the groundwork for my identity as a writer. Thank you!

Thanks to my daughters, Ellie Ryan and Neva Ryan, for all your love and support. I love you so, so much!

Most of all, thanks to David Ryan. Here's to many more years of asking, "You getting anything done?" and "More coffee?" In this case, words are not enough. Maybe I should draw a picture? It's so much easier!